THE FORTRESS

The tall, bald-headed overseer said, "Why have you only brought nineteen slaves?"

"There were twenty when we set out." Niall had counted them.

The man shrugged. "I suppose a spider got one of them."

"You mean one has been eaten?"

"You're lucky you didn't get eaten yourself."

SPIDER WORLD

It's *their* planet now . . . or is it?

"THE SPIDER WORLD SERIES COULD EASILY BE-COME A CULT!" —*Western Morning News*

COLIN WILSON

Colin Wilson is the author of more than fifty novels, plays and essays. His first book, *The Outsider*, was greeted with extraordinary critical acclaim. His work covers a wide spectrum of topics—from philosophy to mysticism, from the criminal to the psychic—and includes *The Occult*, *The Psychic Detectives* and *Poltergeists!*, as well as the science fiction classics, *The Mind Parasites* and *Life Force*.

D1600280

COLIN WILSON

SPIDER WORLD
BOOK THREE
THE FORTRESS

ACE BOOKS, NEW YORK

SPIDER WORLD: THE FORTRESS

An Ace Book/published by arrangement with
the author

PRINTING HISTORY
Grafton edition published 1987
Ace edition/July 1989

ISBN: 0-441-77813-5

Ace Books are published by The Berkley Publishing Group,
200 Madison Avenue, New York, New York 10016.
The name "ACE" and the "A" logo are trademarks
belonging to Charter Communications, Inc.

PRINTED IN THE UNITED STATES OF AMERICA

10 9 8 7 6 5 4 3 2 1

ACKNOWLEDGMENTS

My chief debt of gratitude is to my friend Donald Seaman, with whom this book was originally planned as a collaboration. The idea was abandoned at a fairly early stage, but I had the benefit of his suggestions and advice throughout. I am also deeply grateful to Professor John Cloudsley-Thompson, England's leading expert on deserts, for his invaluable advice on the first section of this book. It also owes a great deal to the warm encouragement of my editor John Boothe.

CW
Cornwall, 1986

For Sally, Damon and Rowan

THE COLD WIND AGAINST HIS FACE restored him to a sense of
normality. He was in almost total darkness. A few moments
later, the moon emerged briefly from behind flying black
clouds, so that he could take his bearings. The grass
underfoot was wet and slippery; it had evidently been
raining heavily. He had to walk carefully to avoid losing his
footing. He held the metal rod by its narrow end, using it as
a staff, and a few minutes later felt the hard pavement under
his feet. The clouds parted again, and the moon revealed the
avenue that stretched northward towards the bridge. He
turned left and walked in the direction of the women's
quarter of the city.

As he crossed to the far side of the square, the wind was
so powerful that he had to lean into it. It was a relief to be
in the shelter of tall buildings. According to his map, this
section of the city was deserted, forming a kind of no-
man's-land between the southern part and the slave quarter.
He paused in a doorway to shelter from the wind, which

made his teeth chatter, and to wait for the moon to emerge. When it did so, he saw something that made his heart contract with fear. The white tower was gleaming in the moonlight, looking as if it was shining with its own inner phosphorescence. And around its base, clearly visible against its whiteness, there was a movement of heaving black shadows. For a moment, he convinced himself that they were cloud shadows; then, as the moon was isolated for a moment in a calm space of unclouded blue, the light strengthened, and he knew they were living creatures. As the light dimmed again, the shadows seemed to be moving across the grass towards him.

His immediate response was to run, but he knew at once that this would be an error. He was already using all his self-discipline to repress the panic; fleeing would amplify it beyond his control. His next impulse was to take refuge in the nearest building. This he also rejected; sooner or later, every building in the city would be searched. The spiders possessed the thoroughness of endless patience. His hiding place would soon become a prison. The correct solution was to keep on the move and hope that the darkness and the wind would delay the search.

He began moving westward, towards the women's quarter, but turned north at each intersection so that he was also moving towards the river. In these narrow, man-built canyons, the darkness was so complete that he had to walk like a blind man, the metal rod stretched out as a feeler, the other hand groping at railings or the walls of buildings. The pavements were cracked and uneven. At one street corner— he could tell it was a corner because the wind converged from two directions—he stumbled over the kerbstone into the gutter, and the rod shot out of his hand. As he groped around on all fours, he had to wrestle with rising panic; the thought of losing the rod filled him with despair. Then he recollected the thought mirror. He reached inside his shirt and turned it on his chest, then sat down in the roaring darkness and concentrated his attention. There was a momentary pain in the back of his skull; then he experienced the sense of power and control. He stood up and spread out his hands within a foot of the ground, walking forward slowly. A tingling feeling in the fingertips of his right hand guided him to the object of his search. Now his mind was calm, it was as if he was able to pick up some faint signal from the metal rod. A moment later, he found it lying in the gutter. He turned the disc again away from his chest, aware of how much this kind of concentration drained his energy.

When the moon came out again, he saw that he had reached a broad avenue. His memory of the map told him that the river was two blocks to the north. He stopped in a doorway and scanned the avenue for moving shadows; it seemed empty. Overhead, a vast spiderweb heaved up and down in the wind; but in such a gale the spider would be crouched in the shelter of some windowless room. Niall hurried on up the avenue; now his eyes were becoming accustomed to the darkness he could move more quickly. In the freezing wind, his face and bare arms were beginning to feel numb. But the cold also brought him comfort; he knew the spiders disliked it even more than he did.

While still a block away from the river, he halted on a street corner to rest. Overhead an immense black cloud covered the moon; he judged that it would take at least ten minutes to pass. He was unwilling to venture on to the embankment in total darkness; if the spiders were guarding the bridge, then it also seemed likely they would be patrolling the river.

He sat on the pavement with his back against the railings of a basement area. Something yielded, and he realised he was leaning against a gate. The thought of sheltering from the wind, even for a few moments, was tempting. He pushed the gate, and it opened with a creak of rusty hinges. Groping on his knees, he felt worn stone steps, slippery with rain. He descended cautiously until he was below street level. There was an unpleasant smell, like rotting vegetation, but at least he was sheltered from the wind. Now his skin was no longer exposed, he experienced an illusion of warmth. He sat there shivering, his arms folded round his knees, and wondered why the smell of decaying vegetable matter seemed to grow stronger.

There was a light touch on his arm, and he started with fear. Since his first assumption was that a spider's fangs were poised to plunge into his bare flesh, he became immobile. The touch groped upward to his shoulder and, at the same time, something brushed the calf of his left leg. As he sprang to his feet, a cold softness closed round his ankle, and the stench of decay was suddenly nauseating. He tore his foot free and felt the same cold softness groping at his arm. Then, as he shrank away, it closed round his upper arm, pulling him against the railing.

In spite of the fear and nausea, it was a relief to know he was not dealing with a spider. These cold, damp feelers moved slowly and deliberately; another was slipping between his legs and winding round his right knee. When he reached down, his hand encountered something cold, soft and slimy; as he squeezed, it seemed to ooze between his fingers. It might have been a cold-blooded worm.

Another of the wormlike fingers tried to pull the metal rod out of his right hand. Niall gripped it tightly and thrust between the railings; he felt it plunge into something soft. Again and again he thrust with all his strength; each time he felt it sink home. Yet the feelers continued to move, groping round his body with unhurried deliberation.

As he felt a cold touch against his face, his loathing turned to cold fury; once again he gripped the end of the rod and thrust between the bars to the full extent of his arm. His hatred seemed to convulse his brain like a shock, and he felt its power rippling through the muscles of his arm and into the rod. He gripped tighter, clenching his teeth, and again felt the shock run down his arm. Suddenly, the feelers released their hold. Niall staggered back against the wall, then clawed his way up the steps and fell out into the street. Coughing and retching, he stumbled forward across the road, then recovered his balance and ran. The cold wind was as welcome as a caress.

Before he had run a dozen yards, self-control returned. He withdrew into a doorway and stood there, eyes closed, resting the back of his head against the wall until his heartbeat returned to normal. His flesh felt sore where the tentacles had gripped him. Finally, to assist his concentration, he again turned the thought mirror on his chest. The pain in the back of his head made him feel sick for a moment; then it passed, and he experienced once more the satisfying sense of being in control of his body and mind.

If the spiders were advancing towards the river, there was no time to lose. He approached the embankment with caution and waited for the moon to emerge. When it did so, it revealed that the great arch of the bridge was surprisingly close, the road that led towards it empty. He waited for the moon to disappear behind the clouds, then crossed the road. A low stone wall, about four feet high, ran along the embankment. He groped his way along this until he encountered a gap. The metal rod, used like a blind man's stick, revealed a recess with a flight of descending steps. He crouched behind the wall until another interval of moonlight enabled him to take his bearings and revealed that the steps were unguarded, then made his way down to the path that ran by the river. Here he became aware of the need for haste. If there were guards on the bridge, a sudden shaft of moonlight could betray him. He hurried forward until the moon showed through a break in the cloud, then halted and pressed himself tightly against the wall; as soon as darkness returned, he went on. Advancing in this way, it took him more than half an hour to reach the bridge. While still fifty yards away, he took refuge behind a buttress and waited until a longer interval of moonlight allowed him to study it carefully. There was no sign of spider guards; but at either end of the bridge were rectangular structures that might have been some form of sentry box. About to move from his hiding place, he obeyed some instinct that urged him to stay still. After a long interval of darkness, moonlight flooded the river, and illuminated the nearest rectangle; it enabled him to see a square window that looked out towards him. And, as he watched, there was an unmistakable movement behind. A moment later, it was blank. But it had told him what he wanted to know: the spider guards commanded a clear view along the river, as well as along the avenue that led to the white tower.

The wind that blew across the river was so cold that he was no longer able to feel his hands or feet. If he remained there much longer, he would probably be unable to move. So as soon as a particularly dark cloud crossed the moon he ran, crouching, until he found himself under the shelter of the bridge. There, concealed by its black shadow, he was finally able to sink down with his back against the wall, huddled into a recess that gave some shelter from the wind, and clasp his knees tightly against his chest in an effort to keep out the cold.

Now, at last, he was able to allow the metal rod to contract and stow it away in one of the pockets of the grey smock. As he did so, he felt the tube that contained the

baggy, metallic garment and experienced a glow of gratitude towards the Steegmaster. This, at least, should provide
some kind of defence against the wind. Very cautiously, he
extracted it and pressed the end with his thumb. As it
unrolled, the wind caught it and tried to tear it out of his
hands, making a loud, flapping sound. Quickly, he thrust it
under his body and sat on it. For the next ten minutes, he
groped in the darkness, flattening the garment against the
ground, holding it down flat with his frozen feet while his
numb fingers tried to unfold it. Eventually, his fingers
located a slide fastener and he realised, to his relief, that
he understood its purpose; the sleep-learning device had
stocked his memory with many such useful items of
information. He opened the front of the garment down to
the waist, then slipped his feet inside. A few moments later,
his arms were encased in the strangely thin material, and the
slide fastener had been pulled up under his chin. The effect
was astonishing. Although the wind continued to press the
material against his bare flesh, none of its cold seemed to
penetrate. He might have been wearing a garment of thick
animal fur. Now only his hands, feet and head were
exposed, and the arms and legs were sufficiently long for
him to be able to retract his hands and feet. Investigation of
a lump at the back of his neck revealed a tightly-rolled
hood; when his fingers had learned the secret of unrolling it,
he discovered that it covered his head completely, and that
a draw-string enabled him to close it until only his nose and
eyes remained exposed. Further investigation revealed similar rolls at the wrist and ankles, but he decided to leave
examination of these until the daylight. It was easier to
exclude the wind by holding the ends of the sleeves with his
fingers and folding the last six inches of the legs under his
feet.

When he once again turned the thought mirror away from

his chest, he was overwhelmed by a wave of fatigue which was transformed into a delicious weariness by the warmth that now encased him. Even the wall behind him failed to communicate its coldness through the paper-thin material. A few drops of water pattered against the suit and made him aware that it was raining; when the moon came out again, he could see the rain falling steadily onto the dark moving surface of the water. But his eyes were unable to focus for more than a few seconds. His eyelids closed and his consciousness merged with the darkness.

When he awoke, the sky over the eastern reach of the river was turning grey. His neck felt stiff where his cheek had pressed against the wall; but the recess had kept him from rolling sideways. In spite of the awkwardness of his position, he felt relaxed and rested. The only discomfort was a cramp in his right leg and the stinging sensations where the tentacles had gripped his flesh.

His stomach was rumbling with hunger; he was just beginning to regret his failure to provide himself with food when he recalled the brown tablets; he unzipped the garment—letting in a wave of cold air—and extracted the box from his pocket. The tablets looked pathetically small, and he was tempted to swallow a handful. He took one and placed it on his tongue. It had an agreeable lemony flavour and quickly dissolved as he sucked it, creating a pleasant sensation of warmth. As he swallowed, the warmth increased until it ran down his throat like liquid fire. A few moments later it reached his stomach; suddenly, the hunger vanished and was replaced by a glowing sensation that felt exactly as if he had eaten a hot meal. He was now glad that he had resisted the temptation to swallow several; more than one would undoubtedly have made him feel sick.

Now it was time to take his bearings. First, he removed the metallic garment, shivering in the dawn wind that blew up the river. He carefully flattened it on the ground, then folded it lengthwise; a touch on the button made it roll itself up into a tube that felt as hard as solid metal. Niall slipped it into the pocket of the grey smock.

Next, he tiptoed cautiously to the west side of the bridge and looked upward. From that position he could see the rectangular guard box; but without moving farther from the bridge, it was impossible to obtain a clear view through its window. He decided that the risk of being seen was too great.

On the other side of the bridge, there was no guard box. Here he discovered a flight of steps leading up to street level. He climbed these warily, pausing for at least half a minute on every step. When his head emerged above the top step, he could see across the damaged bridge to the opposite bank. The guard box was a small, open-fronted building which contained only a stone bench; in the days when this city had been inhabited by men, it had evidently been a pedestrian shelter. The wolf spider inside it was crouched against the wall, and was so completely immobile that Niall had some difficulty in detecting its presence. As Niall watched it, he induced in himself a sense of deep calm; he was more likely to betray his presence by the movements of his mind than by those of his body. He deliberately made himself as immobile as the spider, ignoring the cold wind that numbed his arms and legs.

Half an hour later, the sun rose above the eastern horizon; its warmth was as delightful as a caress. As he sighed with relief and pleasure, he experienced an overwhelming sense of pure wellbeing. It was accompanied by a curious sensation, as if something inside him was dwindling and contracting to a point. As this happened, the pleasure became almost intolerable, and he had to close his eyes to prevent himself from being swept away by it.

As he did this, the feeling of inner-contraction came to a halt, leaving him in a condition of deep calm such as he had never experienced in his life. It was then that he became aware of the thought processes of the wolf spider on the other side of the road. Its awareness was also as still as a candle flame on a windless night. A man who stood in that draughty sentry box would experience boredom and impatience. The wolf spider would have regarded such feelings as a kind of mild insanity. It knew that it had to wait there until its relief arrived, and impatience would have been irrelevant. The sun filled it with a drowsy delight; yet its underlying vigilance remained unaffected. To his surprise, Niall realised he experienced no hostility or fear towards the spider; only a friendly sympathy with a strong overtone of admiration.

The warmth caused a pleasant tingling sensation in his bare shoulders and the calves of his legs, and this again seemed to lift his mind like a wave and move it gently towards some deep source of peace. Now it was as if his hearing had suddenly been sharpened a hundredfold, and as if he could hear a kind of whispering sound. For a moment, this puzzled him; then he identified its source. It was coming from a great elm tree standing fifty yards away along the riverbank. With a shock, he realised that the elm was alive: not simply alive in the negative sense of burgeoning wood and leaves, but in the sense of a being of flesh and blood. The tree was waving its arm in welcome to the sun, and exuding a feeling of gladness that had a totally human quality. All its leaves were rippling with pleasure as they absorbed the golden light, as if they were children shouting for joy.

Now that he was aware of the "voice" of the tree, Niall began to recognise a still deeper undertone of communication. It took him some time to realise that this was coming from the earth beneath his feet. He had to make a mental effort to deepen his inner calm still further; as he did this, he could sense waves of energy rippling past him, like the ripples on a pond when some child has thrown a stone into the water. The tree was receiving this energy and was, in turn, transmitting its own personal response. Suddenly, Niall understood why the city was surrounded by green hills and woods. They focused the waves of energy that flowed through the earth and gave back their own vital response. The result was that this city of concrete and asphalt was pervaded by an aura of living energy. Now he could understand why the wolf spider could wait so patiently for hour after hour. It was not, as he had assumed, simply that spiders are born with the gift of patience; it was because it was aware of itself as a part of this pulsating pattern of vitality.

What intrigued Niall was the sheer intensity of this vital pulse. Now he had become aware of it, it reminded him of the rhythmic burst of rain-carrying wind he had experienced in the storm at sea: curtains of rain blowing across the boat in explosive gusts. But unlike the wind, whose gusts were due to the motion of the ship in the waves, these surges of vital energy produced an impression of purpose, as if generated by some intelligent agency. For a moment, he even speculated whether its source might be the Spider Lord himself.

At this point he became aware of a change in the pattern of consciousness of the wolf spider. With a feeling like waking from deep sleep, he returned to his superficial level of everyday awareness. The spider had been stirred into activity by the approach of its relief. Niall noted with interest that the guard was still inside its sentry box, so that its relief was beyond its field of vision; yet without moving out of the box, it was aware of another wolf spider proceeding along the avenue that led to the white tower. By once again relaxing his attention, he became aware of the nature of this awareness. The approaching relief caused small subsidiary "pulses" in the larger pulsation, disturbing its natural rhythm.

Now there was no time to lose. It was broad daylight and further delay would be dangerous. He slipped quietly back down the stairway and under the bridge. The river lay about four feet below the path on which he had spent the night. A bank of grey mud, about six feet wide, shelved down into the water. Niall slipped off his sandals—they were the ones he had brought from Dira—and tucked them into the wide pockets of the smock. Then he lowered himself off the stone ramp and down onto the mud. It was hard, and his feet scarcely made an indentation. A moment later, he was wading slowly into the water.

Here the mud was softer, and had an unpleasant, slimy consistency; unused to wading, Niall experienced a flash of alarm as his feet sank into it. At each step, his feet squelched down into the mud to a depth of almost a foot. Some small living creature writhed between his toes, and he had to suppress a gasp of alarm. He stood still, trying to control the pounding of his heart. What alarmed him was the realisation that the bright sunlight would make him visible to any creature on the bank of the river, and that the longer he spent wading across, the greater the chance that he would be noticed. For a moment, he was tempted to return and spend the day hiding in the recess; then he saw that this would be even more dangerous, since he would be clearly visible from the opposite bank. He waded on steadily until the water came up to his armpits. Here the current was stronger than he expected, and he was forced to lean sideways to maintain his balance. Suddenly, the bottom was no longer under his feet, and he was floundering. His first impulse was to try to go back, but he saw this would be pointless; safety lay in going forward. He dog-paddled a few feet, then felt himself sinking; as the water entered his nose and mouth, he panicked for a moment, then struggled to the surface, coughing and choking. What terrified him was the thought that the current might carry him out beyond the shelter of the bridge and leave him totally exposed. He thrashed forward a few yards further, then, with relief, felt the slimy mud under his feet again. He stood there for perhaps a minute, simply to regain his breath and to try to get the panic under control, then again plunged forward towards the bank. A few moments later, he was crossing the hard mud that sloped into the water. But he was aware that he had lost the battle against panic.

He resisted the temptation to pause and regain his breath by leaning on the stone parapet; instead, he scrambled up and made straight for the flight of stairs at the side of the bridge. He had already mounted the first half dozen steps when he became aware that it was too late. The wolf spider was waiting for him at the top, its fangs fully extended. The enormous black eyes were staring down at him without expression.

As he obeyed his impulse to flee, the force of its will struck him in the back, knocking him breathless. He had some vague thought of taking refuge in the river, hoping the spider would not dare to follow him. But even as he reached the edge of the parapet, the spider's fast-moving body struck his own and hurled him down on to the mud. His knees and elbows sank in, making movement impossible. As the spider's weight landed on his back, time seemed to move into a lower gear, and he felt himself struggling in slow motion, observing the terror of his physical being as if watching a stranger. Then his face was pressed into the mud and he felt himself losing consciousness.

He woke as if from a nightmare and realised that he was lying on his back. His eyes were blinded by the sunlight. As he thought of the spider, he flung up his hand to defend his throat, then realised he was alone. He looked up, expecting to see the spider watching him from the parapet; there was no living creature in sight. He struggled to his knees, then to his feet, fighting off waves of nausea. It cost an immense effort to drag himself up on to the stone ramp. Still fighting the desire to retch, he crawled across to the wall and collapsed with his back against it.

It was then that he remembered the thought mirror. He reached inside his shirt and turned it round. The effect was instantaneous: that curious sense of concentration and wellbeing that was like being *reminded* of something. But by now, he had become sufficiently accustomed to its properties to observe them with a certain precision. First, it was as if his heart contracted with a feeling not unlike fear. Yet because this contraction was accompanied by a feeling of increased control, it produced a flash of joy, of strength. This seemed to spread instantaneously to the viscera, where it blended with a more physical form of energy. Then the brain itself seemed to unite these two, exactly as if it had turned into a hand that was compressing some tough but yielding material. If he was tired, this action of the brain lacked force and he experienced a twinge of pain behind his eyes. This is what now happened. Then the power of the brain—which he recognised as the mind itself—increased its control, and the headache vanished. And now it felt as if three beams of energy, from the heart, the head and the viscera, were converging on the mirror, which reflected them back again, redoubling their intensity. He could also see—in a brief flash of insight—that the mirror was not necessary. It was merely a mechanical substitute for *self-consciousness*.

As strength and vitality were summoned from his own depths, he tried to understand what had happened. Why was he still alive? Probably because the Death Lord had given orders to capture him alive. Then where was his attacker? Could it have gone to summon the other guard? But he was immediately struck by the absurdity of this explanation. What would be easier than to bind his hands and feet and carry him away on its back?

He stood up and felt the back of his neck. It felt sore and bruised, but there was no puncture mark there. Hope began to dawn. For some reason beyond his comprehension, the wolf spider had left him unharmed. Could it be through the intervention of the Steegmaster?

Cautiously, he mounted the steps again, this time to street level. Wet marks from his previous ascent were still on the stone, revealing that he had been unconscious for only a brief period. He raised his head and peered out across the bridge. It was deserted; so were the streets of the slave quarter. He was about to make a run for the nearest building when he caught a glimpse of the caked mud on his arms and changed his mind. His present state made him too conspicuous. He stood there for perhaps a minute, scanning the street and embankment for any sign of movement; when he had assured himself that they were deserted, he hurried back to the river. There he waded in up to his knees and washed off the mud from his arms, legs and face.

It was as he was wading back on the foreshore that an absurd idea flashed into his head. He was looking at the marks made by the impact of his own body when he fell from the ramp; the indentations produced by his knees and elbows were clearly visibly. Also imprinted in the soft mud were the claw marks of the spider as it had stood above his body. On the left hand side, four marks were visible; on the

right, only three. His attacker was a wolf spider with a
missing front claw.

With a clarity amounting to a perception, Niall's mind
conjured up an image of an exhausted wolf spider lying
sprawled in the sunlight, a trickle of pale blood running
from its maimed foreleg on to the deck of the ship, and he
suddenly knew beyond all doubt that his intuition had found
the answer. Pleasure and gratitude rose in him like a bubble.
The perception that luck was on his side produced a curious
inner calm. He mounted the steps unhurriedly, looked to
right and left to make sure that the road was empty, then
crossed the street like a man going about his legitimate
business.

The houses facing the river had been impressive structures, now crumbling into disrepair; the cracked pavements
were covered with a debris of broken glass and decaying
concrete. Here also he saw for the first time the disintegrating shells of rusty automobiles, many with helicopter
attachments that gave them the appearance of dead winged
insects. In the southern part of the city, most windows and
doors were still intact; here the window apertures were
empty and the doors that remained hung off their hinges.
The slave quarter looked as if it had been vandalised by an
army of destructive children.

The main avenue, which ran down from the bridge, was
overhung with cobwebs, which in places were so thick that
they seemed to form a canopy; an instinct warned Niall not
to venture beneath them. Instead, he entered a building
whose worn façade still carried an inscription: Global
Assurance Corporation, and picked his way across a grimy
marble floor littered with lath and plaster, and down a series
of corridors that led into a narrow street. He peered out
cautiously and withdrew his head immediately; about thirty
feet above his head, a death spider was repairing its web.

He blocked the flash of alarm before it began and retreated into the corridor.

The nearest room contained some broken furniture and its door had been propped against a cupboard next to the empty window aperture. By moving into the space between the door and the cupboard, Niall was able to command a good view of the street and to watch the spider in its patient work of repair. Half an hour later, he heard the first sounds of life: voices, the sound of footsteps and the banging of doors. Across the street, he could see people moving about behind the first-floor window aperture. A woman with large breasts and grotesquely thick legs strolled down the street, making soft crooning noises. He noticed that she walked under the spider web with no sign of nervousness.

The noise increased and as the sun rose high enough to penetrate the narrow street, children appeared on the pavements, many of them chewing lumps of grey-coloured bread. Some of them shouted, or ran about, laughing; most seemed to be quiet and apathetic. Niall observed the prevalence of low foreheads, flat cheekbones and narrow, slit-like eyes. One heavily-built boy with a club foot approached a small fat girl and tore her food out of her hand. She began to wail loudly, but no one paid any attention; the boy leaned against the wall a few feet away, and ate the bread. Then he approached another child who had just walked into the street, and once again snatched the food from her hands. This child tried to snatch it back; whereupon the boy pushed her in the chest with such force that she staggered across the road. Yet other children sat in doorways or on the edge of the pavement and went on eating stolidly, making no attempt to hide their food.

One small boy ran down the middle of the street, flapping his arms as if he were a bird, and making chirping noises. As he ran under the newly-repaired cobweb, he paused and looked up at it. Then, to Niall's astonishment, he bent down, picked up a piece of wood, and hurled it into the air. It curved downward again long before it struck the web. The child threw it again; this time it went slightly higher. Then the boy with the club foot, who had finished eating, picked up the wood and hurled it with all his force into the air. This time it struck the cobweb, and stuck there. Then, so quickly that it made Niall start, the spider fell from the sky on its length of thread and pounced on the small child. Niall expected to see the fangs sink into the bare flesh. Instead, the child shrieked with laughter as the spider rolled him on the ground; many other children joined in. And a few moments later, the spider rose into the air on its lifeline of web, while the child jumped up and ran away. Niall found it all totally baffling. The spider had obviously been playing with the child.

Niall's damp clothes were becoming uncomfortable, and when a child peered in through the window and stared at him with curiosity, he decided there was no point in further concealment and walked out into the street. No one paid him the slightest attention. The spider overhead had now started to build another web, apparently oblivious to what was happening below. Only the boy with the club foot gave him a glance that made him feel uneasy—a look that was at once hostile and mocking.

The thought mirror sharpened his senses, making his observation preternaturally keen. He noticed that the slave quarter was full of smells, both pleasant and unpleasant; the smells of cooking mingled with the odour of rotten fruit and sewage. The gutters were full of abandoned scraps of food as well as all kinds of domestic rubbish. There were also, he soon discovered, nonhuman inhabitants of the slave quarter. As a child threw down a large piece of bread, a bird swooped past his head and snatched it up. And in a shadowy, deserted alleyway, he saw a large grey rat feeding on a smashed watermelon. It glanced at him with its sharp little eyes, decided he could be ignored, and went on eating. A fraction of a second later, a spider plunged from the sky and landed squarely on the rat; the animal had time only for a pathetic squeak before the fangs plunged home. A few seconds later, spider and rat had vanished. It had all happened so swiftly that Niall had no time for fear, or even astonishment. He glanced up nervously at the overhanging web, into which the spider had vanished, and hurried on.

Passing an open doorway a few moments later, his nostrils detected a more sinister smell—rotting meat. He paused, hesitated, then stepped into the shadowy interior, treading with caution on broken floorboards. The source of the stench was immediately apparent—a decaying corpse lying in one corner of the room. It was little more than a skeleton, a few disintegrating fragments of grey slave garments covering the rib cage; maggots crawled out of the empty eye sockets. The cause of death—a great block of masonry that had fallen through the ceiling—lay close to the cracked skull. Niall repressed a desire to be sick and hastened back into the street.

The slave quarter was dirty, overcrowded and apparently totally disorganised. Many buildings were burnt-out shells; others looked as if a vigorous push would bring their walls tumbling down. Inhabited buildings were easy to distinguish because they were in a less dangerous state of disrepair than the others. He strolled into one of these, pushing his way among squabbling children, and was ignored. A doorless room to the right was obviously a bedroom; the floor was covered completely with greasy mattresses. In another room, people sat on the bare floorboards, or on broken furniture, and drank soup out of chipped crockery or gnawed rabbit legs or chunks of grey bread. It was easy to locate the kitchen simply by tracing to its source the pervading smell of burning fat, woodsmoke, garlic and overripe fruit and vegetables. An enormous saucepan of soup steamed on the wood stove; the cook, a grotesquely fat woman whose forearms were thicker than most men's thighs, was chopping up a mixture of fruit, vegetables and rabbit meat on a large board; as Niall entered, she poured these into the saucepan, scraping them off with a carving knife. Two late risers came in, yawning and rubbing their eyes. They helped themselves to unwashed dishes piled up in a metal sink and, without the preliminary of washing them, dipped them straight into the cooking pot; neither seemed concerned that their bowls contained a proportion of raw meat and vegetables. They hacked themselves bread from a loaf that was more than four feet long, and dipped this into a wooden bowl of half-melted butter that stood on the windowsill catching the full force of the morning sun. Niall observed that there was a large metal bunker containing various kinds of fruit: apples, oranges, pomegranates, watermelons and prickly pears. The slaves were obviously kept well fed.

A tall, red-headed man entered the kitchen. Niall guessed he was a member of the servant class condemned to work as a slave. He looked harassed and irritable. Ignoring Niall, he snatched a bowl from the sink, washed it under the tap and filled it with soup. Unlike the slaves, he took the trouble to dip the ladle to the bottom of the saucepan. Niall tuned in to his mind—he found that the thought mirror made this easier than usual—and discovered that the man was entirely preoccupied with the fact that he had overslept, and that in ten minutes time he had to report for work. The man—whose name was Lorris—hacked a chunk of bread off the loaf and began to eat ravenously. His mood was so sour and hostile that Niall was glad to withdraw his mental probe—

the man's state of mind produced an impression exactly like an unpleasant smell.

As he emptied his soup bowl, Lorris seemed to notice Niall for the first time. He asked:

"What are you here for?"

Niall thought quickly. "Arguing with a commander. What are you?"

"Constant lateness." He refilled his soup bowl.

Niall said: "I've only just arrived. Is there anyone in charge?"

"Morlag, in building K.2."

"Where is that?"

He gestured. "Along the street and first left."

"Thank you."

Out in the street, he noticed that many slaves were now walking in the same direction. But attempts to probe their minds were frustrating. There seemed to be almost no mental activity in the normal sense. They were living according to a mechanical routine, and each one seemed to regard himself as a mere fragment of a crowd. They moved like sleepwalkers. It was not unlike being among a pack of human ants. As they passed the house where Niall had seen the corpse—the smell of rotting flesh seemed stronger than ever—none of them seemed in the least concerned that one of their number had been killed. Each seemed to feel that it was none of his business. They were totally self-absorbed.

As he made his way through the crowded streets, Niall was struck by the sheer physical variety among the slave class. Unlike the servants and the commanders—who were united by a strong family resemblance—the slaves seemed to be of every shape and size. Many, but by no means all, were physically deformed. Some looked alert and intelligent, some sullen and bored; a few looked dreamily contented. The alert and intelligent ones were usually small and deformed, while taller, more physically attractive slaves often wore a blank, imbecilic smile. Niall noticed the same anomaly among the women, many of whom stood in windows or doorways and watched the men go past; those who looked alert were mostly short and ugly, while tall, attractive women stared blankly into space, apparently hardly conscious of their surroundings. He was struck by the large proportion of women in an advanced stage of pregnancy, and also by the enormous number of children, many of them leaning dangerously out of upstairs windows. The slave quarter seemed to contain more children than adults.

He found himself in a small square in which several platoons of slaves had already lined up. A big, black-bearded man of tremendous physique stood facing them, an expression of grim disgust on his face. The noise was deafening; children shouted and played games, adults screamed at one another, while two very pregnant women fought and rolled in the gutter. Niall approached the black-bearded man.

"I'm looking for Morlag."

"That's me. What do you want?"

"I've been told to report to you."

Morlag suddenly roared "Shut up!" in a voice so deafening that it struck Niall like a physical blow. Instant silence fell on the square, and the squabbling women let go of each other's hair and sat up. Morlag said: "That's better. Any more noise and I'll feed you all to the spiders." He looked down at Niall, whose face was on a level with his chest.

"Why did you get sent here?"

"Arguing with a commander."

Morlag grunted: "Serves you right." The noise had already started up again. "What job do you do?"

"Charioteer."

"All right. Wait there." He pointed to the pavement behind him where four more powerfully-built servants were standing.

A twinge of pain in the back of Niall's skull reminded him that he had been using the thought mirror for too long. He reached cautiously inside his shirt and turned it over. The sense of relaxation was so powerful that for a moment he felt dizzy and had to close his eyes. And even before he opened them, he was once again pervaded by that sense of total calm he had experienced earlier by the river. His own identity seemed to fade away and he became a part of the communal life that surged around him. He was simultaneously inside the minds of all these people in the square, sharing their sense of absurd wellbeing. He was also aware once more of the rhythmic pulse of life that moved in periodic waves through the earth under his feet, like a rising tide gently breaking on a beach. The slaves were also dimly aware of this pulse, and it intensified their joy in being alive.

Niall's four companions, on the other hand, were totally unaware of it; their minds were entirely preoccupied with which jobs the overseer would assign to each of them. Niall's insight into their minds intrigued him. He could sense that they all regarded it as a humiliation to be condemned to live among slaves, and that this fostered an attitude of resentment towards the spiders. At the same time, each felt that his position had important compensations. Among their fellow servants they were nonentities; here they were regarded almost as gods. They had first choice of the best food, were waited on hand and foot and allowed to take their pick of the most attractive slave women. All this had developed in them a certain spirit of independence; none of them really wanted to be sent back to live among fellow servants. Potentially, such men were allies against the spiders.

At the moment, their attitude towards Niall was unfriendly; he was a stranger, and he might be assigned one of the more desirable jobs. The most coveted assignments were farm work and food gathering, which allowed an unusual degree of freedom. On the other hand, everybody hated street cleaning and sewage work, since these involved working under the direct observation of the spiders. For some reason, working for the bombardier beetles was also regarded with deep distaste.

When Niall turned his attention to Morlag, he realised with dismay that the overseer intended to assign him to take charge of a street cleaning detail. That would be a disaster; he would be recognised as soon as he crossed the bridge. For a moment, he considered the idea of slipping quietly away, then dismissed it; Morlag would want to know what had happened to him. The alternative was to try to influence the overseer's mind, to implant the suggestion that he should be assigned to some other detail.

Niall stared at the back of Morlag's head, at the same time reaching inside his shirt and turning the thought mirror. But even as his fingers touched it, he realised that this was not the answer. The thought mirror reflected his powers back inside himself and so diminished his power to influence other people. It was as he turned it back again that he made another discovery: as the mirror turned, it was as if his focused attention was deflected away from himself in a concentrated beam. Suddenly he understood. When the mirror was turned inward, it intensified his thoughts and feelings. When it was turned outward, it could be used as a reflector, beaming his thoughts and feelings towards other people. He had only to direct his own concentration towards the mirror.

He tried it, staring intently at the back of Morlag's head. The result surpassed his expectation. Morlag was halfway through a sentence, roaring "Stand to attention and get in line, you stupid . . ." Then his voice faded, and a blank expression came over his face. He shook his head as if an insect were buzzing around it, and tugged nervously at his beard. Niall's companions gazed at him in astonishment, wondering what had happened. Then Morlag seemed to recollect himself. "Time to get started. You . . ." He turned to the nearest servant. "Take this lot to the rabbit farm. You and you, report to the main square for street cleaning." His attention came to rest on Niall. "You . . ." His memory seemed to fail him for a moment, and in that moment, Niall selected from his mind the assignment he preferred. "You, report to the bombardier beetles. You, take this lot to the sewage works . . ." As he passed on down the line, Niall averted his eyes to conceal his relief.

Five minutes later, Niall was marching north along the main avenue, at the head of a squad of twenty slaves.

THE DAY WAS BRIGHT AND CLOUDLESS, and the north-east wind had the refreshing coolness of early morning. Accustomed to the hot, dry wind of the desert, Niall found it intoxicating; even the slight dampness of his clothes against his skin gave him pleasure. Ahead of them, the avenue stretched in a straight line towards the green hills in the distance. The sight of them brought a curious elation, a sense that freedom lay on the other side.

Most of the buildings on either side of them were in ruins; some were fire blackened shells, with trees and tall purple weeds pushing their way out of doors and windows. Overhead, the thick, dusty cobwebs were less dense than in the city centre. Niall experienced a continuous sense of observation from unseen eyes; it was as if he were being lightly brushed by beams of intense curiosity. He deliberately kept his mind closed, refusing to allow his consciousness to reflect anything but his immediate surroundings.

A mile or so further on, the scenery changed; ruined skyscrapers and tower blocks gave way to smaller buildings, many surrounded by tangled wildernesses of greenery; this had evidently been a residential area of the city. Soon the webs disappeared as the gaps between buildings became too wide to be bridged with spider silk. Here, at last, Niall felt able to relax, and to give free rein to the thoughts and feelings that filled his being with excitement. Again and again he reached inside his shirt and turned the mirror; each time, he experienced the surge of delight and incredulity as he felt his mind concentrate like a compressed spring, then release its energy in a brief surge of power. It was astonishing to feel that his mind had exactly the same power as his hands: not merely to grasp, but to *change* things.

It was, of course, the same power that the spiders possessed. And once again he was overwhelmed by that staggeringly simple yet fundamental insight: that men have become slaves of the habit of changing the world with their hands. The spiders had the tremendous advantage of never having formed that habit.

Suddenly, it seemed preposterous that men had been on earth for so many millions of years without discovering the true use of the mind. And horribly tragic that some of them—like the slaves—had literally lost their minds, like deep sea fish who have lost their eyes . . .

The thought of the slaves made him look round. They had ceased to march in ranks and were shambling along with bowed shoulders; some stragglers were fifty yards behind. Niall concentrated his will and sent out a beam of command. The result astonished him. The nearest slaves staggered, as if struck by a powerful blast of wind; those farther away jerked frantically to attention. All looked shocked and bewildered. Niall tried again, this time more gently. The slaves immediately closed ranks, threw back their heads and began to march like trained soldiers. Niall himself felt curiously exalted by this response and experienced an answering surge of vitality. For perhaps five minutes—until the attention of the slaves began to waver— he felt as though they were all part of a single organism— perhaps some enormous centipede marching on its multiple army of legs.

Abruptly, the buildings came to an end. From the top of a low rise, they found themselves looking down on open countryside, and on cultivated fields with barley and green vegetables. They passed an orchard where slaves were gathering fruit, tended by an overseer who might have been Odina's sister. Aware of her expectation, Niall saluted her smartly, and made the slaves do the same. Her amazement warned him that this was a mistake, and he made a mental note to avoid flamboyant gestures.

A mile further on, the road entered an area of dense woodland whose emerald green foliage overhung the road. Niall found it so enchanting that he allowed the slaves to break ranks and slow down to a leisurely stroll. There was a point where a small stream ran beneath the road, rippling over lichen-stained pebbles. The slaves ran down into this and splashed through the shallow water; as they did so, Niall's own feet and ankles became almost painfully cold.

As they emerged from the woodland Niall saw, at the foot of the hills to the north-west, a series of red towers like twisted church spires. He turned to the nearest slave, a gangling, cross-eyed youth with a hare lip. "What is that?"

"Crashville."

"Crashville?"

The youth nodded delightedly, and shouted: "Boo-oom!" at the same time waving his arms upwards to simulate an explosion. The other slaves began to chuckle and giggle, repeating "Boo-oom!" in intonations that varied from a low roar to an excited shriek. Crashville must be the slaves' nickname for the city of the bombardier beetles.

Half an hour later, they were met by a tall, bald-headed man who wore a yellow tunic and green eyeshade; his face was red and harassed.

"Where have you been? You're late!"

Niall said: "I'm sorry. They won't walk very fast."

"Where's your whip?"

"I'm afraid I don't have one."

The man groaned, and cast his eyes up to heaven. "Here, borrow mine." From a large pocket of his tunic he pulled a coiled leather whip. The slaves eyed it nervously.

"I don't think I know how to use it," Niall said.

"I'll soon show you." He uncoiled the whip, cracked it, then went behind the slaves and slashed at the ankles of the stragglers. They closed ranks and broke into a trot. The man followed them for a few yards, swearing and cracking the whip, then slowed down to a walk beside Niall.

"See? That's the only way to do it."

Niall said humbly: "I see."

"Why have you only brought nineteen?"

"There were twenty when we set out." Niall had counted them.

The man shrugged. "I suppose a spider got one of them."

Niall was appalled. "You mean one has been eaten?"

The man looked at him pityingly. "You're new at this, aren't you?"

"Er . . . yes."

"You're lucky you didn't get eaten yourself. Oh well, I suppose we can make do with nineteen."

Now they were entering the city of red towers. Each tower was an immense spiral cone and seemed to be made of a waxy, shiny substance; it was as if some giant had seized each while it was still soft and given it a clockwise twist. Through the door in the base of the nearest tower, Niall could see an ascending ramp. There were window-like apertures in the twisted sides, and from the highest of these, just below the apex of the tower, a bombardier beetle goggled down at them. Around the foot of the tower was a moat about two feet wide, and in this, a small beetle, hardly more than a baby, was floating on its back, its silvery green belly exposed to the sunlight.

This colony of the bombardier beetles consisted of several hundred of these towers, spaced at wide intervals on smooth green turf. Between were low, one-storey buildings made of a blue substance like opaque glass, and with small circular windows like portholes; these were evidently the homes of the human servants. Like the towers, the houses were surrounded by neat green lawns, intersected by water channels and by paths of a pink material like marble. Children dressed in yellow tunics broke off their play to stare at them curiously as they passed. Attractive women, many with spinning wheels, sat in the shade of blue glass porches. Most of them wore their hair very long—in some cases, below the waist—or piled in coils on the top of the head.

"Who lives there?" Niall asked. He pointed to a tower at least twice as high as the others.

"Nobody. That's the town hall."

They entered the central square, a smooth rectangle of green turf neatly intersected by paths. Niall could now see that the central building consisted of two halves: a blue glass structure surmounted by a red tower. An impressive flight of curved steps ran up to its main entrance.

The slaves, who had evidently been here before, had drawn up in ranks at the foot of the steps. The bombardier beetles who wandered in and out of the building ignored them. As Niall and his companion approached, a man in a shabby yellow tunic emerged from the main entrance and walked down the steps; even at a distance, Niall recognised the spindly legs and beaky nose. He was about to smile and wave when Doggins looked directly into his eyes. To Niall's surprise, he showed no sign of recognition; instead, he looked away and addressed Niall's companion.

"You'd better get a move on or we'll be late starting."

"That's not my fault. This chap"—he glanced pityingly at Niall—"forgot to bring his whip."

"That was careless." Again, Doggins looked at Niall as if he had been a stranger. "All right, get 'em over to the quarry."

"Right, Cap'n." The bald-headed man saluted, then beckoned to Niall. "You, come with me."

Doggins said quickly: "No, I'll be needing him for the next hour or so. You go ahead with this lot. And don't let 'em get near the fireworks." He turned his back on them, saying casually over his shoulder: "You—come this way."

Niall followed him up the steps. They entered a large, dim hall whose cool blue light was welcome after the blaze of the sun. Bombardier beetles and their servants bustled about them, the beetles towering above the humans. Niall sensed about them that same indifferent friendliness he had perceived in the camel spiders of the desert. Without glancing back, Doggins led him across the hall and pushed open a door labelled: Director of Explosives. The room had no windows, but a cool blue light filtered through the walls, creating a curiously soothing effect. Doggins flung himself into an armchair behind a huge desk and glared at Niall.

"Well, you're about the last person I wanted to see."

Niall, who had been hoping for a friendlier welcome, said: "I'm sorry."

"You bleedin' well ought to be. What are we going to do with you?"

Niall said apologetically: "You don't have to do anything with me. I'm supposed to be in charge of the slaves."

"I know that. And where will you go tonight?"

"Back to the slave quarter."

Doggins stared at him incredulously. "You must be crazy. They're all looking for you. We had 'em here first thing this morning."

Niall asked quickly: "What happened?"

"What do you think? We've promised to look out for you and send you back if we catch you."

"And are you going to?"

Doggins shrugged irritably. "Now look, son, you'd better get one thing clear. We've got an agreement with the crawlies—live and let live. If we gave you shelter, and they found out, it'd be war. And we just can't risk that. I shouldn't even be talking to you now."

Niall stood up. "I'm very sorry. I don't want to get you into trouble. I'll go away."

Doggins' glare became less pugnacious. "Where do you think you're going?"

"I'll hide somewhere until it's time to go back."

Doggins grunted. "There's no point. They won't be back looking for you. You'd better stick around here and act normal. And if anybody asks, I don't know you. Right?"

Niall nodded. "Right."

Doggins stared into his eyes for a long time. He said finally: "So they found out."

"Yes."

"I warned you about that." He gnawed his lower lip. "They'll kill you if they find you."

"I know."

There was another long silence. Then Doggins said: "Your only hope is to get back to your own country. We might be able to smuggle you across on one of our boats."

Niall said: "It's very kind of you. But I don't want to go back. I can't leave my mother and brother behind."

"You can't help them much if you're dead."

"I'm going to try to hide in the slave quarter."

"They'll find you sooner or later."

"Perhaps. But I can't just give up. I've got to try."

Doggins shook his head with exasperation. "Try *what*? What are you hoping to achieve?"

Niall met his eyes. "To destroy the spiders."

Doggins smiled pityingly. "And just how do you propose to set about that?"

"The spiders aren't physically stronger than we are—they just have a stronger will-power. And that's no different from having stronger muscles. We could fight them if we used our intelligence."

Doggins regarded him thoughtfully. "Yes, now I can see why they think you're dangerous."

It made Niall realise that, without intending it, he had been concentrating his attention through the thought mirror; the result was that his words struck Doggins with immense conviction. He pressed the advantage.

"You could blow up the whole spider city with your explosives."

"Of course we could—if we had enough explosive. But we wouldn't, and they know we wouldn't."

"Why?"

"Because we're the servants of the beetles, and the beetles would never order us to do it."

"But why should you be a servant? Men were once lords of the earth."

Doggins gave a snort of laughter. "And a right bleedin' mess they made of it! Do you really want to know why the crawlies don't like human beings? Come with me and I'll show you."

He stood up and led Niall out into the hall. It was totally empty. They climbed a short flight of steps and halted in front of a door made of gold-coloured metal. Doggins pulled this open and beckoned Niall to go inside. The room beyond was dark.

A moment later there was a tremendous crash, and a blinding flash of light. Niall jumped backwards and cannoned into Doggins. Doggins gripped his elbow.

"Steady. It's all right. Just stand quietly."

Still trembling with shock, Niall stared with horrified amazement. The opposite wall had turned into a vast expanse of blue sky, with fleecy white clouds, and across this expanse, machines that he recognised as aeroplanes hurtled with a shrieking roar that deafened him. Suddenly, the view changed; he was looking down from an aeroplane, watching egg-shaped objects fall towards the ground. They continued to fall until they diminished into dots and disappeared. Then, from the ground below, there was a series of white puffs, one after another, in a straight line. This time the explosions were distant and muffled.

Once his eyes were accustomed to the semi-darkness Niall could see that he was in another large hall. In front of him was an audience of bombardier beetles; he could sense their breathless attention. Now it dawned upon him that the scene he was watching was not some form of magic. A cone of wavering light overhead told him that it was merely an illusion, projected onto a wall-sized screen.

Doggins grasped him by the elbow, steered him into the semi-darkness and indicated a chair. Without taking his eyes from the screen, Niall sat down. He was witnessing a bombing raid on a large city, and the destructiveness took his breath away. He watched tall buildings shudder, then crumble slowly to the ground, sending up a cloud of dust. Fire exploded in clouds of red and yellow, then merged into a whirlpool of black smoke. Firemen directed jets of water into the flames; then another building collapsed and buried them.

Doggins whispered in his ear: "This is just an old movie, not the real thing. The real thing comes later."

Niall said: "It's horrible!"

"Don't let them hear you say that. They think it's marvellous."

The screen went blank for a moment; then there was a burst of loud marching music, and a man's voice announced impressively: "Demolitions!" There was a sibilant stir of applause from the audience; this was clearly a favourite. A semicircular tower block appeared on the screen, photographed from below so that its walls seemed to rear up like the sheer face of a cliff. Then, by some trick of photography, the camera moved slowly into the air and rose towards the roof of the building; the time it took to do this emphasised its enormous height. Finally, the camera was looking down on it from above. It pulled back to a safe distance. Niall held his breath. There was a puff of smoke at one corner of the building, then a second. At the third puff, the walls began to crumble; slowly, the walls cracked and buckled; a cloud of dust went up at the base as the building disintegrated into falling masonry, then subsided into a heap of rubble. Niall had to admit that there was something magnificent about the spectacle.

The remainder of the film followed the same pattern; skyscrapers, building developments, factory chimneys, even cathedrals, all collapsed into the same cloud of smoky dust. And as each one crashed to the ground, there was a sibilant hiss of applause from the beetles—they seemed to make the sound by rubbing their feelers together.

For Niall, this was a shattering experience. By turning the thought mirror towards his chest, he was able to absorb its full impact and appreciate it as a reality. His vision in the white tower had enabled him to grasp something of the extent of human destructiveness. But this unending panorama of violence made him aware that he had not even begun to grasp its enormity. There was old footage of the First World War, showing the artillery bombardments that preceded an attack and disembowelled bodies sprawled on the barbed wire; there were newsreels of the blitzes of the Second World War, and of dive bombers strafing undefended cities. There was archive material of the dropping of the first atom bombs on Japan, then of the testing of the hydrogen bomb on Bikini atoll. As the smoke cloud rose above the ground and revealed that the atoll had ceased to exist, even the beetles seemed too stunned to applaud.

Doggins nudged him in the ribs. "Seen enough?"

"I expect so." But he kept his eyes on the screen until they found themselves outside in the blue daylight; there was something hypnotically fascinating about the violence. It was a strange sensation to find himself out in the empty hall, like waking from a dream.

As they walked into the sunlight, Niall had to shield his eyes. After the cool of the building, it was like stepping into a hot bath.

"How long does that go on?"

"For the rest of the afternoon. We've got about two hundred hours of film footage."

"Haven't they seen it all before?"

"Dozens of times. But they never get tired of it."

The green lawns with their neatly symmetrical buildings seemed somehow unreal. After the unending thunder of explosions, the peace seemed to hover over them like a threat.

They had crossed the square diagonally and were approaching a house that stood on the corner. This was notably larger than those that surrounded it, and a fountain played in the centre of the lawn. About a dozen children were dangling their feet in the green water; several of them had the distinctive Doggins nose. When they saw Doggins, half a dozen children rushed across the grass and flung their arms round him, clamouring to be picked up. A pretty, dark haired girl came out of the house.

"Let daddy alone. He's busy."

Reluctantly, the children returned to their bathing pool. To Niall's surprise, the girl seized both Doggins' hands and kissed them. Doggins looked embarrassed. "This is my wife Selima."

Niall felt a twinge of envy; the girl was scarcely older than Dona. He held out his hand to clasp forearms and was startled when she dropped onto one knee, seized his hand, and kissed the palm.

Doggins cleared his throat. "Let's have something to eat."

"Yes, Bill." She vanished into the house. Doggins said awkwardly: "Very affectionate girl."

As they entered the house a voice called: "Who is it?"

"It's me, my love."

A large handsome woman with platinum blonde hair looked out of a doorway. She also seized Doggins' hands and kissed them. "This is my wife Lucretia," Doggins said.

The woman gave Niall a brilliant smile; the blue light of the hallway made her teeth look like precious stones. "His first wife," she said.

Niall, slightly taken aback, smiled awkwardly.

Lucretia asked: "What is his name?"

Doggins said: "Er . . . Mr. Rivers."

"Is he a Bill?"

"No, no, just a mister."

"What a pity." She disappeared through the nearest

doorway. Niall caught a glimpse of a kitchen, in which several girls were preparing food.

Niall was puzzled. "What did she mean—am I a Bill?"

Doggins chuckled. "I've told 'em that Bill means 'a man of power and magnificence.' She was paying you a compliment."

He led Niall into a large comfortably furnished room. A slim, bare-armed girl who was sitting on the couch jumped to her feet and kissed his hands. Then, as Doggins sat down, she knelt and pulled off his sandals.

"This is Gisela," Doggins said, "—she's number eight. This is Mr. Rivers, my pet."

The girl glanced shyly at Niall, averted her eyes, and blushed. Niall guessed she was even younger than Dona. She asked her husband:

"Shall I wash your feet now?"

"No, pet, just get us some cold beer."

"Yes, Bill." Niall observed that she spoke his name with a certain solemnity, as if saying "lord."

When they were alone, Doggins gave him a roguish grin. "Now you can see why I don't want to get mixed up in any war with the crawlies?"

Niall said sadly: "Yes."

"It's not that I don't want to help you. But you couldn't win anyway." When Niall made no reply, he went on: "I mean, let's be realistic. There's millions of spiders. What can any of us do against that kind of odds?"

Niall shook his head stubbornly. "There *must* be a way. Otherwise they wouldn't be afraid of us. Why *are* they afraid of us?"

Doggins shrugged. "Because we're a bloody destructive lot, that's why. You've seen the films."

"Then why aren't they afraid of you? You know the secrets of explosives."

"Why should they be? I'm doing all right. In ten years' time I could even be the General Controller."

The platinum blonde came into the room followed by several girls carrying trays. She moved a low table between Niall and her husband and spread it with a white linen cloth. As she poured the beer, she asked:

"Had a good morning, dear?"

"So so. You know what Boomday's like."

"What did those spiders want?"

"Oh, they were looking for a runaway slave."

"A slave? All those spiders? What had he done?"

Doggins avoided Niall's eyes. "I don't know. They didn't tell me."

The table was now laden with many kinds of food: oysters, mussels, quails' eggs, small roast birds and several varieties of salad and vegetable. The beer was dark brown and slightly sweet—and, as Niall realised after drinking down half a glass to quench his thirst, very strong. Before they ate, the girls held out bowls of warm water for them to wash their hands, then dried them on towels that were as soft as eiderdown. After this, the women quietly withdrew.

For the next five minutes both of them devoted their full attention to the food. Niall was experiencing a feeling of romantic melancholy that was not entirely unpleasant; the sight of so many young girls reminded him of Dona, and made him aware that he was missing her.

Doggins was obviously thoughtful. As he ate the quails' eggs with a rich white sauce, he wore an abstracted expression. Periodically, he glanced at Niall from under lowered eyebrows. He said finally:

"Look . . . suppose we *could* make a deal with the spiders . . . I'm not promising anything, but just suppose we could? Wouldn't that solve your problem?"

"What kind of a deal?"

"Well, suppose they'd agree to let you come and work for us?"

Niall asked cautiously: "What makes you think they'd agree?"

"They owe us a few favours." He bit into a roast lark. "As I see it, they're worried because they're afraid you're a troublemaker. Right? And if we could guarantee"—he laid special emphasis on the word—"that you wouldn't make trouble, it's just possible they might do a deal."

"And I'd live here . . . and work for the beetles?"

"Well, you'd be working for me. I need a new assistant. Do you know anything about explosives?"

"I'm afraid not."

"That doesn't matter. You'd soon learn." Doggins became mellow and expansive. "Gunpowder's easy—saltpetre, sulphur and charcoal—you just have to get the proportions right. Dynamite's a bit more complicated—my last assistant blew himself up when he was making nitroglycerine. But you wouldn't be doing that. Your first job would be to distil the coal tar products." And, between mouthfuls of food, he began to explain the principles of fractional distillation.

Although Niall appeared to listen attentively, his mind was elsewhere. He found it hard to believe that the spiders would allow him to become a servant of the beetles. Yet Doggins seemed confident enough. The idea was certainly tempting. He could think of nothing more delightful than living with Dona in a house like this. The mere thought was enough to send him into a romantic daydream.

Doggins drained the last of his beer, pushed back his chair and stood up. He patted Niall on the shoulder. "Don't worry, lad. Doggins the Powerful and Magnificent has a certain amount of influence. Now I'm going to get changed. Help yourself to beer."

Niall was glad to be alone; it gave him a chance to collect his thoughts. What worried him now was what would happen if the spiders learned his whereabouts. If he was recaptured, he would be worse off than before. If they didn't kill him, they would make sure that he never had another chance to escape. So could he risk allowing Doggins to try and negotiate for him?

And even if the spiders allowed him to go free, would he really be so much better off? The beetles were allies of the spiders. To work for them would be almost as bad as working for the spiders.

The more he thought about it, the less he was able to see any solution. He wandered restively around the room, his hands in his pockets, pausing every time he passed the window to stare at the fountain. Now the children had been called indoors, it looked oddly desolate, its spray rising into the sunlight as if trying to escape into the sky, then curving back to earth, like his own thoughts . . .

His attention was attracted by a persistent tingling in the fingers of his right hand; his fingertips had been toying with the telescopic rod. He took it out and weighed it meditatively in the palm of his hand, deriving a curious sense of comfort from its weight. Then, pressing the button that made it expand, he was struck by the intensity of the tingling sensation that communicated itself to his slightly damp skin; the vibration was stronger than he had ever known it. Holding the rod between the thumb and index finger of either hand, he concentrated all his attention on the vibration.

With a clarity that made him jump, the voice of the Steegmaster spoke inside his chest.

"Tell him about the Fortress."

For a moment, Niall's mind was a blank. He asked in bewilderment: "Fortress?" He had already forgotten what

the word meant. But even as he spoke, the tingling
sensation faded. He stared down at the rod, confused and
disappointed, and wondering whether he should try to
renew the contact. At that moment, he heard the sound of
Doggins' voice in the corridor and pressed the button that
made it contract. As Doggins came into the room, he
dropped the rod into his pocket.

Doggins looked unexpectedly impressive. Instead of the
shabby yellow smock, he wore a black toga, with a gold
chain round the waist. The leather sandals were also black,
and on his head, in place of the battered green eyeshade, he
wore a black peaked hood which gave him a monkish
appearance.

"Ready? We'd better get a move on."

Outside in the corridor, the women and children were
waiting, all dressed in gaily coloured clothes. The only
exception was Lucretia, who wore a black linen toga,
evidently to emphasise her position as wife number one. As
Doggins and Niall marched out into the sunlight, the family
walked behind in an orderly crocodile, the tallest at the
front, the smallest in the rear.

They crossed the green in front of the town hall and
turned into the extension of the main avenue. Every
inhabitant of the town seemed to be going in the same
direction, the emerald-backed beetles with their bright
yellow heads towering above their human servants and
conversing among themselves in sibilant squeaks. The
humans were excited and boisterous, and if noisy children
occasionally cannoned into the legs of the beetles, no one
seemed to mind. Niall was struck by the friendly and
easygoing relations that seemed to exist between the beetles
and the humans; unlike the spiders, these huge, armour-
plated creatures seemed to inspire neither fear nor vener-
ation; only affectionate familiarity.

As they left the square, Niall suddenly remembered the word he had been trying to recall. He asked Doggins:

"What's a barracks?"

"It's a place where soldiers live. Why?"

"I saw the word on an old map."

Doggins glanced at him quickly. "Of the spider city?"

"Yes."

Doggins asked casually: "It wasn't called the Fortress, by any chance?"

"Yes, it was. How did you know?"

Doggins shrugged. "I've heard rumours about it. Do you think you could describe where it is?"

"I think so. It's in the slave quarter."

They had reached the outskirts of the town, and Niall was interested to see that one of the red towers was under construction, and that a large cloud of golden insects was swarming and buzzing over the unfinished walls. He asked: "What are they doing?"

"Building it."

Niall asked in amazement: "The insects?"

"That's right. They're called glue flies."

As they came level with the truncated tower, the buzzing noise was deafening. Niall shouted above the din: "Are they building it for themselves?"

"Oh no." Doggins halted and his retinue of wives and children also came to a stop. "They live in nests made of leaves stuck together with glue."

"Then how do you make them build houses?"

"They're specially trained. Watch." He twisted his face into a scowl, wrinkled his forehead and glowered at the swarming golden insects through narrowed eyes. After a moment, they began to settle on the walls; at the end of thirty seconds, the buzzing noise had ceased, and the insects were crawling over one another's backs. Drops of sweat were standing out on Doggins' face. He gave a gasp and relaxed; instantly, the insects were in flight again. Doggins looked pleased with himself.

"How did you do that?"

"They're trained to respond to mental orders. Why don't you try it?"

Niall stared at the glue flies and concentrated his attention. He was instantly aware of the presence of each individual insect as if they had become a part of his own body, like his fingers or toes. He was even aware of their precise number: eighteen thousand, seven hundred and eighteen. But as he was about to transmit the mental order for them to settle, he recalled his earlier resolve to avoid flamboyant gestures, and changed his mind.

"I'm afraid I don't seem to be able to do it."

Doggins smiled sympathetically, but with a trace of satisfaction. "No, it takes a lot of practice."

And now, as they walked on, Niall became aware that the moment of empathy with the glue flies had established a sense of contact with the stream of life that flowed around him. It was astonishingly different from the feeling he had experienced that morning, standing in the square among the slaves. Then he had been conscious of a kind of mindless wellbeing. Now he was aware of being amongst others like himself, human beings with the same power to think and control their own lives. There was only one difference: they were not aware that they possessed this power.

He asked Doggins casually: "How did you learn to control the glue flies?"

"Oh, it's not difficult. They're used to being controlled by the beetles. I've been with the beetles so long that I suppose I'm on the same mental wavelength, so I can do it too . . ."

He was wrong, of course. It was nothing to do with

mental wavelength; it was purely a matter of will-force. For a moment, Niall felt tempted to explain, then decided that this was neither the time nor place.

Half a mile beyond the edge of the town, the road turned a corner, and Niall suddenly found himself looking down into an immense hole in the earth. It must have been a mile wide and a quarter of a mile deep. The drop made him feel dizzy.

"What is this?"

"An old marble quarry."

"But what made it?"

Doggins grinned. "Human beings."

In its sheer sides, Niall could see the layered geological strata, the broadest of which was the same colour as the road under their feet. This was obviously the source of the road-building material.

The road descended into the quarry in the form of a gentle ramp; bombardier beetles and human beings poured down it in a gaily coloured stream. On the floor of the quarry he could see dozens of coloured tents, one of which—striped in green and white—was far larger than the rest. He could also hear a sound that made his heart lift in sudden gaiety: the noise of brass musical instruments played in unison.

It took them nearly half an hour to descend to the bottom. There were still many large pools of water from last night's rain, and children ran barefoot through these and shrieked with laughter as they splashed one another; other children were gathered around a Punch and Judy show. Pleasant smells of cooking and burnt caramel blew towards them from the coloured tents and booths. The members of the brass band, dressed in bright red togas with yellow sashes, stood on a platform of natural rock, and an amphitheatre behind them amplified their sounds like a powerful loud-speaker.

This end of the quarry was dominated by a grandstand with perhaps a thousand seats and covered by a transparent dome like a green-tinted bubble.

Doggins said: "If you want a good view of the show, try and get a seat on the top row. It starts in about half an hour. Now I'm going to leave you—I've got things to do."

"Thank you." Niall was looking forward to exploring the sideshows.

But a moment later, Doggins was back. He said quietly: "Trouble."

Niall followed the direction of his gaze and felt his heart sink. Among the crowds descending the ramp was a group of bare-breasted women; he recognised them immediately as commanders. For a moment he experienced panic.

"Do you think they're looking for me?"

"No. They often come here on Boomday."

"What shall I do?"

"Don't worry. I don't think they'll recognise you. To them, you're just another slave. But you'd better keep out of sight."

He pointed to the striped marquee which faced the grandstand. "You'll find the slaves working in there. You already know Mostig—he's the bald-headed man you met this morning. Go and ask him if there's anything you can do."

Niall entered the marquee and found it a chaos of activity. Most of the floor space was taken up by an elaborate stage set, which represented an island covered with trees. There was a ship at anchor on imitation blue waves, and nearby a creek ran into the sea. The beach was covered with native straw huts, and a witch doctor with a necklace of skulls was dancing round a cooking pot that contained an unhappy-looking sailor. On closer examination, Niall discovered that the witch doctor, like the island itself, was made of wood and papier mâché, much of it still being painted by the stage hands.

The rear of the marquee, which was open, faced the wall of the quarry, and Niall could see that it was supported by a complex arrangement of ropes and pulleys. Immediately behind the marquee, a cave had been hollowed out of the rock face; in front of this, slaves were loading a cart with barrels. The bald-headed man, looking exhausted and harassed, seemed to be trying to supervise everybody at once. When Niall asked him if there was anything he could do, he snapped irritably: "Just go away." Then he looked closer and said: "Oh, it's you. I could have done with your help a couple of hours ago. Where have you been?"

"Helping Mr. Doggins."

"Well go and try to make those slaves hurry up. Here, take this." He handed Niall his whip.

Niall made his way into the cave. This sloped back far into the cliff and was packed from floor to ceiling with wooden kegs and ammunition chests. One of the kegs had smashed open on the floor, and the cross-eyed youth was trying to sweep up the gunpowder with an absurdly inadequate broom. Niall could see at once that the problem was not to persuade the slaves to hurry, but to induce them to slow down. They were all wildly excited by the carnival atmosphere, and were rushing backwards and forwards like demented termites, rolling barrels and dragging ammunition cases, then forgetting what they were supposed to do with them and leaving them where other slaves could trip over them. A red-headed youth with knobbly knees, evidently the bald-headed man's assistant, was doing his best to control them but finding it beyond his powers.

Niall introduced himself and ascertained precisely what had to be done. Then he organised the slaves into teams of three and allotted each a separate task. He pretended to make use of his whip; in fact, it was unnecessary. The slaves responded to a concentrated effort of will with a readiness that reminded him of the glue flies. One team fetched kegs from the back of the cave, another loaded them onto small wheelbarrows, while a third wheeled them into the marquee. There they were packed by stage hands into a hollow space underneath the island. Within a quarter of an hour, the work was completed, and the bald-headed man began to look at Niall with a new respect. When Niall asked if there was anything more he could do, he said: "Just keep those bloody slaves out of the way until we're ready to start."

At that moment, Doggins came in through the front entrance of the marquee; as Niall waved to him, he frowned and shook his head imperceptibly. A moment later, Niall understood the reason. Immediately behind Doggins were half a dozen commanders, and the woman walking in the forefront of the group was Odina. Fortunately, her face was turned away from Niall as she spoke to the woman behind her. Niall turned and hurried out of the rear entrance.

The gunpowder cave was now deserted; the broken barrel, with its scattered grey powder, still lay in the middle of the floor. Niall made his way past it to the rear of the cave. Here it was pleasantly cool and smelt of damp fungus. After the turmoil of the marquee, he was glad to relax. He chose a dark corner behind a pile of barrels and sat down on an ammunition case. After a few moments, he allowed his eyes to close and leaned his head back against the wall.

A light touch on his cheek jerked him to wakefulness. He sat up with a gasp of alarm and peered into the shadows. There was a slight movement, and for a moment he thought he was looking at a small millipede. Cautiously, he moved a powder keg to admit the daylight. There was nothing there but a yellowy-green fungoid growth, like a distorted mushroom, growing out of the wall. He took the telescopic rod out of his pocket and poked at it; it seemed quite solid. He wondered if some small creature could be using the fungus as a shelter, and prodded it with his finger. As he did so, a tiny grey pseudopod, like a moist finger, emerged from the edge of the fungus and tried to touch his hand. Instinctively, Niall drew back. Then, since the pseudopod seemed as harmless as a worm, he held out his finger again and allowed the creature to touch it. To Niall's amazement, the pseudopod suddenly became thinner and longer and, with a movement of lightning swiftness, wrapped itself round his finger like a tiny coil of rope. He reached out with his other hand to feel its texture; another pseudopod snaked out from the fungus and gripped his finger. He tugged gently, and felt them tightening their grip. They were trying to tug his hand back towards the fungus. He gave a sudden sharp tug, and pulled his fingers free. Each had a tiny red band where the tentacles had gripped.

This was obviously a smaller version of the creature he had encountered the night before: the same cautious, tentative probing movements that reminded him of the horns of a snail, the same slimy grip that was able to exert a surprising amount of force. He pushed the telescopic rod under the fungus and levered it away from the wall. It seemed to be attached by a central root; but at the base of this root was a circle of tiny orifices, like small hungry mouths, when he pushed the tip of his little finger against one of these mouths, it opened immediately and sucked in the finger, while half a dozen grey pseudopods reached out and tried to grip his hand. They seemed to emerge from the slimy surface of the fungus, as if it was composed of some viscous liquid. When Niall tugged his hand free, the tip of his finger was covered with a slimy substance that stung; he wiped it clean on his smock.

As he stared at the grey pseudopods, he deliberately relaxed and allowed his mind to become totally receptive. He was attempting to discover whether the creature was an animal or a plant. For a moment, his own brain seemed to share its famished and predatory consciousness; then his mind slipped beyond it and he became aware of a sensation of gently pulsating energy, as if he were looking at the creature through the ripples on the surface of a pond.

"What are you doing?"

The voice was as startling as a sudden blow. He had been so intent on the fungus that he had not even noticed Odina as she approached him on bare feet.

She repeated: "What are you doing?"

Niall found his voice. "I'm hiding."

"I can see that. From what?"

His anxiety gave way to a mixture of relief and guilt. The relief was due to the startling recognition that she was glad to see him. The guilt came from his immediate and instinctive violation of her mind. He knew her so well that it seemed completely natural to enter the privacy of her thoughts, yet as he did so, he felt like a thief entering her bedroom.

He made room for her on the ammunition chest, and she sat down beside him; he was not sure whether the suggestion came from his own mind or from hers. He looked into her face for a moment; then, with the same instinctive impulsion, took her in his arms and kissed her lips. Her arms went round his neck and they clung together. It seemed completely natural, and both experienced a feeling of relief and delight that it had finally happened. He also became aware that she had been wanting him to do this since she had caught him kissing the dark-haired girl in the women's quarter.

She was the first to break away; the trained commander in her took over.

"What are you running away from?"

"I had to get away from the city."

"But why?" She was obviously baffled. To her, the spiders were stern but benevolent masters, and it was a privilege to serve them.

"They killed my father."

"I know that. It was unfortunate. But he tried to attack one of them."

"I know. But I still find it hard to forgive."

"You *have* to forgive. They are the masters. We have no right to criticise anything they do."

It was strange talking to her like this; he could see her words forming in her mind before she spoke, so there was an odd delayed-action effect as she voiced them. For a moment, Niall was tempted to tell her what Kazak had told him; then he dismissed the idea. It would be unfair to her to allow her to know too much. Her mind was not prepared for such a burden.

She said gently: "You must return with me to the city. They will understand why you ran away and will forgive you." Her arms tightened round his neck so he could no longer see her face. "Then you can become my husband."

It was, Niall realised, an extraordinary offer, like a princess offering to marry a farmhand.

"A commander cannot marry a runaway slave."

She took his face between her hands and looked into his eyes. "A commander can marry anyone she likes—that is her privilege."

She kissed him again, this time very gently, but maintaining the contact for a long time. Something seemed to pass from her lips into him, and from his lips into her—an exchange of vital energy. It was then that Niall realised she had left him without alternatives. It was true that he could easily persuade her to go away and pretend she had never seen him; because she loved him, she would do whatever he asked. But if he did so, he would be turning her into a traitor, and she would feel overwhelmed with guilt. He knew that would be impossible; she filled him with a feeling of protectiveness.

He said: "Very well. I will do as you ask."

This time she tightened her arms round his neck and kissed him hungrily; both abandoned themselves to the pleasure of this exchange of living warmth. Then Niall felt something brush his hair and started with disgust as a pseudopod started to explore his neck. She asked: "What is it?"

He pointed. "What is that?"

She laughed. "Only a squid fungus." She stood up, drew a dagger from her belt and slashed the fungus. It fell on to the floor. To Niall's surprise, she bent down, impaled it on her dagger, and dropped it into a leather pouch at her waist.

"What are you going to do with it?"

"They are good to eat." She caressed his hair. "When you are my husband, I will cook them for you." From outside, the brass band played a fanfare. "Now we must go." She took his hand.

"Is it a good idea for us to be seen together?"

She laughed. "Why not? It will make the others jealous."

As she drew him out into the sunlight, Niall experienced a mixture of delight and sadness: delight at being with Odina, sadness at knowing that his attempt to escape had been a failure.

Doggins, who was standing at the rear of the marquee, looked at Niall with astonishment and consternation. Niall avoided his eyes.

The grandstand was now full, the humans tightly packed

on benches, the bombardier beetles standing on broad platforms between the rows. Odina led Niall to a bench that was evidently reserved for commanders; she sat down and made a place for Niall at the end. The other commanders glanced at Niall with mild curiosity, and he was interested to observe that none of them seemed to guess his identity. Odina had apparently kept her secret from them.

On the row in front of them, the whole Doggins family stared at the marquee with fascinated absorption, the children all sucking large and brightly coloured lollipops. From inside, the green-tinted bubble dome looked blue, its glass so perfectly transparent that it was almost invisible; it seemed to have the property of cutting out the heat of the sun, transforming the midsummer heat into the pale warmth of a winter afternoon.

Odina was talking to the girl sitting next to her. Niall looked at her with a certain pride. With her honey-coloured hair, her sunburnt breasts and her white teeth, she was by far the most attractive of the commanders. Happiness had given her an inner glow. Was Niall in love with her? The question was almost irrelevant. He was at the age when everyone wants to fall in love, and would have been willing to consider any girl who showed signs of being susceptible to his attraction. As far as Niall was concerned, the question of whether he was in love with her was secondary to the fact that she seemed to be in love with him.

The band blew another fanfare. There was instant silence, everyone's eyes on the marquee. Slaves were pulling out the pegs that held it against the ground. Bill Doggins stepped forward, bowed to the audience, then turned to the marquee and flung his arms above his head with a gesture of command. The marquee rose slowly into the air, sweeping back towards the cliff on its hidden pulleys, then was lowered over the gunpowder cave to form a backcloth.

Cheers and clapping broke out at the sight of the island. Doggins, having established himself as the donor of the entertainment, moved gracefully to one side. Then a black-bearded pirate captain stumped onto the deck of the ship on his wooden leg, glared out ferociously at the audience, and roared: "Avast, ye lubbers, I can see ye watching me! You don't frighten Pegleg Pete!" He turned and shouted down below: "Men, there's a crowd of idiots out there staring at us! Let's go and cut 'em to pieces!" At that moment, there was a loud explosion from behind him, and Pegleg Pete leapt into the air like a startled roebuck, losing his hat and telescope in the process. The audience roared with laughter, and the beetles made a curious quivering motion and rubbed their feelers together, making a sound like crickets. Niall, for whom pantomimes were only a distant racial memory, laughed louder than anyone.

The entertainment proceeded. Pegleg Pete and his crew had come to the island in search of buried treasure; Pete said he was hoping to retire on the proceeds and become a hangman in his spare time. But the island was full of murderous cannibals (played by the slaves, with blackened arms and faces). Pete's new Master of Artillery—the last one had been eaten by a shark—was an incompetent who could not strike a match without causing an explosion. When the captain ordered a false distress signal to lure a passing merchantman into an ambush, and the Master of Artillery acquiesced with a cross-eyed leer, all the children shrieked with laughter, knowing the result would be yet another disaster. When the Master of Artillery emerged on deck a moment later with an armful of skyrockets, the entire crew—including Pegleg Pete—dived for cover, and the laughter and stamping of feet was so loud that Niall had to cover his ears. Inevitably, the rockets exploded in all directions, and the Master of Artillery turned a spectacular backward somersault off the deck, escaping injury by a miracle of timing. He was evidently a trained acrobat.

There was a love story, which Niall found even more absorbing than the periodic explosions. The second mate, an honest young fellow who had been captured by the pirates in a skirmish, fell in love with a beautiful lady on the plundered merchantman, and they decided to escape. Seized by cannibals, they were forced to watch from behind prison bars as the natives prepared a feast at which they were to be the main dish. Fortunately, their captors were unaware that the fuel they had gathered for the fire included a bundle of signal rockets. In due course, the fire exploded, the cannibals fled, and the prisoners escaped. Now Niall understood why they were enclosed in the bubble dome; three of the rockets struck it with tremendous impact and exploded without even leaving a mark.

In the third act—the pantomime lasted almost two hours—the mate and his lady love were tied to the masts of the pirate ship, with kegs of gunpowder around them primed to explode, while the captain and crew prepared to escape in the merchantman. The cannibals chose this opportunity to raid the pirate ship. While the hero, with incredible dexterity, cut the bonds of his lady love with a dagger held in his teeth, the cannibals swarmed aboard up a rope ladder. Since the slaves had been insufficiently rehearsed, there was a failure of timing, and the cannibals stood around in a circle, watching the hero's contortions while he did his best to ignore them. Doggins could be seen standing in the wings, waving his arms, but no one paid any attention. Finally, the two principals were freed, and the hero cut the burning fuse with his dagger and tossed the spluttering end over his shoulder. Inevitably, it landed in a bucket of signal rockets, which flew off in all directions, their sparks igniting fireworks which—for unexplained reasons—had been left lying around the deck. This was plainly the build-up to the climax. As the hero and heroine rowed away to safety—pulled by an unseen rope—the ship turned into a spectacular firework display with coloured sparks pouring out of its portholes, its hatches and even the tops of the masts.

At this point, it became clear that the cannibals were not obeying their instructions; they were dancing around joyfully in the showers of sparks, laughing and waving their arms. One of them gave a roar of pain as a rocket soared between his legs, and leapt overboard; but the others seemed to be enjoying themselves too much to be afraid. Doggins finally rushed out from the side of the stage and shouted at them, but his voice was drowned by the crash of fireworks and shrieks of laughter.

It was then that the first explosion occurred; the fo'c's'le of the ship suddenly disintegrated into matchwood. The slaves fell silent and stared with amazement, almost as if they thought it was a joke. In the momentary silence, the voice of Doggins could be heard shouting furiously: "Get out of there you fools!" Then he turned and fled as a tremendous explosion rocked the boat.

Black smoke poured up from the decks and a shower of debris rattled down on the bubble dome. The children in front of Niall were clapping and cheering with excitement, apparently assuming that this was all part of the entertainment. Fireworks were exploding all over the island, and Niall observed with misgivings that the marquee suspended against the cliff had caught fire and was dissolving in an upward surge of flame. The island itself exploded in an ear-splitting roar; as it did so, Niall remembered the gunpowder scattered on the floor of the cave. A second later, the grandstand rocked back and forth as the earth shook, hurling children to the floor. Women began to scream, then to cough and choke as black smoke billowed under the bubble glass dome. The trembling was like an earthquake; fragments of rock pounded down on to the dome like black hail. Some of the seats collapsed; most of them seemed remarkably stable. One huge piece of rock, as large as a man, smashed its way through the bubble glass, splintering the steps below Niall. But most of them caused only star-shaped cracks in the glass, which, in spite of its transparency, was obviously as strong as steel.

Surprisingly, there was no rush to escape; everyone realised they were safer inside. The children below cowered on the floor, staring up at the glass above them as it was darkened with falling rubble. Odina had seized Niall's hand and buried her face against his shoulder. The crashing and shaking gradually receded like thunder, until all was still again.

Niall said: "I'm going to see if Doggins is all right." He made his way down the stairs, clinging onto a rail and skirting the hole that had been made by the falling rock. The smell of dust and sulphur dioxide was choking so that he was unable to swallow. It was like walking through a heavy fog. As the dust settled, and the sunlight revealed what had happened, Niall realised how lucky they had been to be enclosed in the bubble dome. All the tents and sideshows had been blown away. Where the island had been, there was a deep crater in the floor of the quarry. And behind it, the explosives cave had disappeared; the cliff above it had collapsed, and there was only a mountainous pile of rubble.

He found Doggins, looking dusty and angry, staring into the crater. Niall said:

"Thank heavens you're all right."

"Oh, I'm all right. But I've lost a hundred bleedin' tons of explosive." He gestured with fury and despair at the pile of rubble.

"What about the slaves?"

Doggins said sourly: "They got what they deserved, bloody idiots. But what am I going to do for explosives for the rest of the year?"

"Hadn't you better go and find your wife? I expect she's worried about you." He could not get used to referring to wives in the plural.

"Yes, I expect so." With a groan of vexation, Doggins turned back towards the grandstand, whose dome was covered with dust and rubble, some of it stained an ominous red. Behind them there was another thunderous crash as a further section of the cliff collapsed.

Mostig, the bald-headed assistant, hurried out from the tunnel under the grandstand; to Niall's surprise he was smiling broadly. He chortled as he patted Doggins on the shoulder.

"Marvellous! You'll get promotion for this!"

Doggins glared at him, evidently suspecting sarcasm. "What are you talking about?"

Mostig lowered his voice. "They think it was all part of the show. I wouldn't tell 'em any different if I was you."

A crowd of bombardier beetles emerged from under the sagging dome and surrounded Doggins. They were waving their feelers and making high-pitched chirping noises, and even Niall could tell they were conveying congratulations. Doggins turned from one to the other with a dazed smile, and waved his fingers with a deprecatory gesture. Niall was puzzled when the largest of the beetles raised his right foreleg and placed it gently on the top of Doggins' head, and Doggins immediately prostrated himself on the ground. He asked Mostig in a whisper: "What docs that mean?"

Mostig was staring so intently that Niall had to repeat the question.

"It means . . . it means he's saying they regard Bill as

one of themselves," Mostig said finally. He seemed unable to believe his eyes.

"And is that a great compliment?"

"Of course it is! It's like being . . . made king."

Doggins was being urged to rise to his feet; he did so with an air of broken humility. For a moment, Niall encountered his eyes and was startled by their anguished expression.

Now the smoke was drifting away; beetles and human beings were issuing from the grandstand. Lucretia, brushing the dust from her black toga, looked on the verge of tears, and an air of dejection hung over the rest of the wives and children. When she saw her husband surrounded by beetles, she looked apprehensive; but as she listened to the high-pitched stridulations, her expression changed to delighted astonishment, then to incredulity. The other wives and the children, realising that something important was happening, also became watchful and silent. Finally, the beetles moved off, and Doggins once more prostrated himself on the ground and remained there until they were out of sight. When he stood up, Lucretia flung her arms round his neck, and the wives and children crowded around him. Mostig muttered in Niall's ear:

"Well, some people are born lucky."

Niall was looking for Odina; a moment later he saw her among the crowd that streamed from the grandstand; it was obvious that she was also looking for him. Niall started to push his way towards her. Before he had advanced more than a few yards, someone gripped his arm. It was Doggins.

"Don't go away. I want a word with you."

"All right. But I have to talk to that commander over there . . ." He waved to Odina but she was looking the other way.

Doggins said: "Later." He seized Niall by both arms and steered him firmly in the opposite direction, towards the platform on which the musicians had been playing. Behind this, they were invisible to the crowd.

"That Fortress—can you tell me where it is?"

"Well, yes. But I'd have to draw you a map."

"Never mind the map. Could you take me there?"

Niall stared at him in astonishment; he thought there must be some misunderstanding.

"But it's in the slave quarter of the city."

Doggins nodded impatiently. "I know that. Can you take me?"

"When?" Niall was thinking of Odina.

"Now—tonight."

"I'm sorry, but that's impossible."

"Why?" It was almost a howl of agony.

"Because I've promised to go back to the spiders."

Doggins shook his arm. "What are you talking about, you idiot? I told you I'd handle that."

"But that was before she found me—the commander over there . . ."

Doggins groaned. "You mean you're under arrest?"

"Not exactly. It's just that I promised her . . ."

"What's going on between you two?" Niall avoided his eyes. "There *is* something going on, isn't there?"

Niall felt guilty on Odina's behalf; he said finally: "She wants to marry me."

To his surprise, Doggins gave a sigh of relief. "Thank God!" He punched Niall on the shoulder. "So if she wants to marry you, she's not going to turn you over to the crawlies, is she?"

"But she wants me to go back, and I've promised . . ."

"That's all right. You can do that tomorrow." His voice took on a pleading note. "You can persuade her. Tell her you've promised to help me this evening. Tell her what you like. She can stay here overnight and you can both go first thing in the morning."

"But why do you need me to go with you? I could draw you a map."

Doggins shook his head. "That's no good. *You* brought the slaves here this morning. So you've got to take 'em back this evening. Right?"

Niall was bewildered. "The slaves?"

"That's right. The slaves." He winked.

Suddenly, Niall began to understand what Doggins had in mind, and it startled him. He turned his face away to conceal the hope that made his heart beat faster; Doggins mistook this for hesitation.

"Come on now. It's not much of a favour."

Niall drew a deep breath. "I'll have to speak to Odina first."

Doggins squeezed his arm. "I'll go and get her."

While Doggins was away, Niall's mind was racing. He found it hard to believe his good fortune, yet his relief was tinged with doubt. For the past few hours he had been wondering how to persuade Doggins to become an ally; now it looked as if he had decided to do it of his own accord. What baffled Niall was why he was prepared to take such a risk.

Odina came alone. As soon as he saw her, Niall knew she would do whatever he asked. He reached out to take her hands; then her arms were round his neck.

"Listen, we are going to stay here tonight," he said. "Are you allowed to do that?" She nodded. "Good. I've promised Doggins, and I don't want to break my word." But he could see that explanations were unnecessary; she would accept whatever he said. "Will the other commanders wonder where you are?"

"No. We are allowed to stay where we like."

As she kissed him repeatedly, with tiny, nibbling kisses, he was struck by an oddly inappropriate image: he was reminded of the tiny grey pseudopodia reaching out to grip his finger. Then he dismissed the notion and gave himself up to the physical relief of feeling her pressed against him.

Doggins appeared round the end of the platform, making them both start. "Sorry about that." He smiled apologetically. "It's time we got moving."

THERE WAS A LIGHT SILVER MIST on the road when they set out, so the rising moon made their shadows seem alive. The air was damp and chilly, and Niall was glad of the inner glow left by the bowl of mulled wine they had shared before they left. He marched in front, while the others followed in two straggling lines. They wore shabby grey smocks, and anyone who passed them on the road would have taken them for an utterly weary band of slaves returning from a long day's work. In fact, the man who marched behind Niall, and who carried his left shoulder higher than his right, was the actor who had played the pirate captain, while the hump-backed youth who shambled beside him was Mostig's assistant, wearing a cushion sewn inside his smock. Most of them were young, having been chosen for smallness of stature.

Progress was slow, for Doggins—who brought up the rear—would not allow them to cover the distance to the spider city at their normal brisk pace; he insisted they should try to think of themselves as tired slaves, and march accordingly. They followed his instructions so conscientiously that it took them almost two hours to cover the distance to the northern outskirts.

Niall, who had at first been doubtful about this venture, began to feel increasingly confident as they approached the city. His main fear had been that these inexperienced youths might betray themselves through anxiety or nervous tension, but he soon realised his mistake. The servants of the beetles had never had reason to be afraid of the spiders, so they regarded this invasion of their stronghold as an amusing adventure. This was why, as he marched through the cold moonlight breathing in the fragrance of leaves and damp earth, Niall experienced the joy that comes from launching into action and knowing that there can be no return.

In fact, the main avenue seemed strangely deserted; the white, broken buildings looked as empty as a desert landscape. This time, Niall experienced no sense of being observed by unseen eyes. If the spiders were watching them it was without curiosity.

Niall and Doggins had already agreed on their plan. Niall would lead them to the small square in which the slaves had gathered that morning. There they would disband and make their way in groups of twos or threes to the barracks, which was only three blocks away to the north-east. They would take refuge in the nearest inhabited house and wait there until all gathered together. Then, in the early hours of the morning, they would make their attempt. Niall reasoned that when the whole slave quarter was asleep, the spiders would have no reason for vigilance.

It was as they began to approach the river that he experienced his first misgivings. Although oil lamps gleamed from behind the cracked window panes, and cooking smells drifted from open doorways, the streets themselves remained deserted. Niall had taken it for granted that the slave quarter would be as crowded during the evening as it had been at dawn. This silence filled him with foreboding. If the slaves were unafraid of the spiders, why were they all indoors?

Niall turned left off the main avenue and a few minutes later brought his squad to a halt in the square. Although this was deserted, the surrounding houses were full of activity; he could hear babies crying and women and children shouting. For the sake of appearances, Niall called out: "Squad halt! Dismiss!"

Doggins sauntered over, hands in his pockets, and indicated the nearest open doorway with a jerk of his head: "That'll do. Let's find something to eat." The march had made them all hungry.

But as Niall attempted to walk into the house a pregnant woman came rushing towards them, waving her arms and shouting: "No room, no room!" She advanced determinedly and forced them to retreat. The door slammed behind them. Niall and Doggins looked at each other in amused astonishment as Niall said: "What now?"

"Let's try next door."

But the same thing happened there. A pale, hollow-chested man with a goitre was sitting at the bottom of the stairs, eating a bowl of soup; as soon as Niall pushed open the front door, he shouted: "Sorry, no room. Try somewhere else." As Niall tried to advance, he jumped up and firmly blocked the passageway. For a moment, Niall was tempted to push him aside, then decided it would be dangerous to attract attention. Besides, it was clear that the man was telling the truth; he could see that the front room was crowded to overflowing.

Outside, Doggins was becoming anxious. In the deserted

square, a group of twenty slaves was conspicuous; it was obviously important to find shelter as soon as possible. But a glance through some of the other lighted windows showed that most of the houses in the square were equally crowded.

The house on the corner bore a rough handpainted sign with the inscription: "K.2." It sounded familiar; then he remembered. This was where he had been told to look for Morlag, the black-bearded overseer. He pushed open the door and was relieved when no one came rushing towards him. But when he stepped into the passageway, a voice from the top of the stairs shouted: "Get out!" A face peered down over the banisters. It was the man called Lorris.

"We've only just got back. Where can we go?"

Lorris recognised him. "Oh, it's you. You can come in. I thought it was a slave."

"But I've got twenty slaves outside. Where can we go?"

Lorris shrugged. "They can go anywhere they like—so long as it's not the same place as last night."

Niall was puzzled. "What do you mean?"

"That's the rule. They're not allowed to spend two nights in the same place."

"Why not?"

Lorris threw up his hands irritably. "How do I know? I didn't make the rule."

"Thanks."

Outside, Niall said: "We'd better move. Let's try the next street."

"Wouldn't it be better to get closer to the barracks?"

"Do you want to risk it?"

"It's better than standing out here." Doggins pointed to an alley at the north-east corner of the square. "Let's go that way."

"It might be better to stick to the main streets."

Doggins shook his head. "Let's take the shortest way. You'd better go first."

Niall decided not to argue. He led them across the square and into the alleyway. But within a dozen yards, the darkness was so complete that they were forced to halt. It was like being surrounded by black velvet curtains. Doggins said:

"Hold on a minute while I strike a light."

Another voice, which Niall recognized as that of Mostig's assistant, said: "What's happening?" Niall thought he detected a note of panic.

Then, quite abruptly, he was gripped by a sense of danger so acute that it made the hair stand up on the back of his neck. It was a sense that they were close to some terrible disaster. He gripped Doggins' wrist. "I think we'd better go back."

"What for?"

"Do as I ask."

They obeyed the urgency in his voice. A moment later, they were back in the square. Mostig's assistant said: "Where's Marcus?"

Doggins said: "Marcus?"

There was no reply. It was then that Niall knew the disaster had already happened.

Doggins went back towards the alleyway, calling: "Marcus." Before he could advance into the darkness, Niall seized his arm and held it tight.

"Don't."

Doggins tried to shake himself free. "For God's sake, I can't leave him to die."

Niall leaned forward and spoke in a low voice. "He's already dead." In his mind's eye, he could see the blackened body of his father.

"Oh Christ!"

Niall could sense his rising panic and grasped the extent of their danger. His own response was to become increasingly focused and controlled. Deliberately using the thought mirror to project the full force of his will, he leaned forward and whispered in Doggins' ear:

"Tell them you've found him. Then say we have to move on."

He could feel the command taking effect, the panic subsiding.

Doggins turned back to the others. "All right, we've found him." His voice was brisk and calm. "Now let's go."

Niall said: "Form ranks and follow me."

To his relief, they obeyed without question. If the moon had been visible, the deception would have been impossible; but it was hidden behind tall buildings to the south-east, and the darkness was almost total. A few moments later, they were marching eastward along the centre of the narrow street.

Niall was shaken. He had no doubt of what had happened. Marcus had been seized in the dark, probably by a spider that dropped from overhead. Any attempt to scream or struggle had been paralysed in advance by the brute force of the spider's will. At this moment, he was probably being eaten. And even now, the danger was not over. If any of the others became aware that Marcus was no longer with them, there could still be an explosion of panic that would betray them to the spiders.

It was only when they marched across the next moonlit intersection, and no one glanced to right or left, that Niall knew he could relax. Doggins had said Marcus had been found, and no one thought of doubting his word.

Niall knew precisely where they were; he could see the map of the slave quarter as clearly as if it had been suspended in front of his eyes. Because it had been absorbed in a state of intensified concentration, every detail was sharp and clear. It showed him that the barracks lay two blocks to the north. The simplest approach would have been via that broad avenue that ran from the town hall to the river, but he rejected this as too conspicuous. Instead, he decided to continue along the narrow street and turn left at the next intersection.

On the other side of the broad avenue they entered an area that had at some time been devastated by fire. Most of the houses were empty shells, and there was a smell of burnt wood in the air. To the south, the moonlight shone on piles of rubble, and beyond that he could catch a glimpse of the river. At the next street, Niall ordered a left turn. Here the houses had also been damaged by the fire, but most were still standing. He experienced relief to see that there were no cobwebs overhead. It seemed unlikely that these crumbling buildings would conceal spiders.

Halfway along the street, a twisted tree was growing out of a ruined building, its branches overhanging the road. The house immediately opposite had collapsed, blocking the street with an irregular pile of rubble which at its lowest point was about six feet high. Niall chose this point to scramble across the barrier, leaning forward to test each step with his hands before entrusting it with his full weight. In this way, he reached the far side with nothing worse than a scraped wrist and bruised ankle, and turned to wait for the others. The moon was directly behind them, silvering the branches of the tree, and he observed that its leaves were rustling gently as if in a breeze.

He had time to register this as odd—since the night was windless—when the spider dropped from the darkness. It happened so swiftly that it seemed a flicker of shadow. There was no sound of impact, only the muffled cry of the man on whom it landed, so faint that none of the others seemed to notice it. While Niall stared for a moment, paralysed by unbelief, he saw the movement of the head that meant the fangs had plunged home. Then he shouted, and the others looked round in alarm. The man attacked had been the hindmost. If Niall had not seen the drop no one would even have noticed that he had disappeared. Now he knew what had happened to the missing slave when they were marching to the city of the beetles.

Without thinking about it, Niall began to scramble back up the rubble, knocking someone off balance as he did so. He reached the top in time to see the spider disappearing towards an open doorway, carrying the man's inert body like a large doll.

His reaction was instinctive; he picked up the nearest large brick and hurled it. It made a soft thud as it struck the hairy body. Instantly, the spider stopped—Niall could sense its astonishment—dropped the body, and turned. Even as the stone had left his hand, Niall had realised it was a rash thing to do; now he tried to turn and run. It was impossible; his body had been immobilised, as if the muscles were encased in a block of solid ice. While the others watched in horror, the spider advanced towards him, its fangs extended; in its blank eyes, Niall could sense the intention to kill. He had committed the unthinkable act of attacking a spider.

Then someone screamed, and Niall realised that his body was not entirely paralysed. The thought mirror was burning his chest as if it had been heated in a fire. As he watched the casually slow movement—the spider seemed to be deliberately taking its time—he experienced a surge of bitter rage at this brutal assumption of total superiority and made a convulsive attempt to tear himself free. The mirror seemed to become painfully hot, so that he was afraid it would blister his chest, and it caused him to intensify the effort.

Then, with the suddenness of a snapping cable, the spider's will seemed to rebound on itself, and it flinched. As this happened, it was struck squarely by the concentrated force of Niall's loathing. It cowered like a dog cringing away from a physical blow. Then its anger overruled its surprise, and Niall again became aware of the full force of its will as it struck back at the control centre of his nervous system.

This time he was expecting it, and fought back. Encouraged by his knowledge that the creature was not invincible, he directed his will as if it was a shout of rage. Again he saw it flinch; yet its will continued to hold him at bay, so his efforts were ineffective, like a man trying to hit something beyond reach. He tried to bear down on the spider, leaning forward as if walking into a gale, and felt that its will was crumbling. Then, with a suddenness that made him stagger, it abandoned the fight. For a moment, its legs seemed to buckle; then it turned and fled, seizing the inert body as it went. Niall experienced a surge of wild exultation, perhaps the greatest sense of triumph he had ever experienced in his life. Then, just as suddenly, he was overwhelmed by an immense weariness that passed downward from his shoulders to his feet. For a moment, his knees buckled, but hands prevented him from falling. By the time he was back on the level ground, the weariness had been replaced by a throbbing headache.

Doggins said: "How did you make it go away?"

"I'll explain later." His tongue faltered, as if he were drunk. "We've got to get out of here."

As they hurried on, he could sense their fear and knew that the danger was greater than at any time since they had entered the slave quarter. If there were more spiders in these buildings, they would be attacked before they reached the end of the street. His own exhaustion made him feel helpless, and he was distracted by the burning pain on his chest. It was this acute physical discomfort that led him to reach inside his smock to feel the area with his fingertips; it seemed to be covered with tiny ulcers or blisters. Then, as an experiment, he turned the thought mirror so that its concave side faced inward. Instantly, the pain intensified so that he gasped aloud; Doggins gave him an anxious sideways glance. For perhaps a minute, his brain was like a boat tossed on a choppy sea of agony. Yet this pain finally succeeded in concentrating his will, and he experienced a sense of re-established control. It was intoxicating, almost as exciting as vanquishing the spider. All his life, he had become accustomed to surrendering to a certain degree of pain or exhaustion. Now he had overruled the lifelong habit and for a moment felt like a man standing on a mountain top.

They had reached the end of the street and found themselves looking across another wide avenue, whose time-blackened buildings appeared at once monumental and shabby. Facing them on the opposite corner was a twenty-foot-high wall, its top surmounted by long spikes. The face of the wall was perfectly smooth, as if it had been cut out of solid rock. It looked as unclimbable as a vertical cliff. In the moonlight, the barracks reminded Niall of the citadel on the plateau.

The others were staring at it with dismay. Only Doggins seemed unconcerned. In his expression, Niall detected a gleam of triumph.

Niall asked: "What are you hoping to find in there?"

"Explosives." He gave Niall an odd sideways glance. "And weapons."

"Weapons?"

Doggins said softly: "Yes, weapons." He turned to the others. "All right. Stick close to me, and try and stay in the shadows."

Within fifty yards they found themselves facing the main gates of the Fortress. There were great solid doors, higher than the walls, and also surmounted by spikes that looked as sharp as needles. Beside them, set in the wall, was a smaller door, also made of the same rusting metal. Half a dozen of them tried to force it with their shoulders, but it was as unyielding as the wall itself.

Another fifty yards brought them to the south-western corner, and to the avenue that ran down to the river. A single glance told them that the west-facing wall was as impregnable as the rest. Unlike the buildings in the avenue, these walls had evidently been built to last for centuries.

Halfway along the north-facing wall, they encountered another entrance. This was a single gate of solid metal, with the usual row of unbroken spikes along its top, and was set between tall pillars, each surmounted by a single spike. Doggins halted and surveyed this with a close attention that Niall found puzzling—it looked as unpromising as any other point of entrance—then said: "Milo, the rope."

One of the men pulled off his grey slave smock; underneath he was wearing the standard yellow tunic of the beetle-servants. From around his waist he uncoiled a length of rope; to Niall's eye it looked dangerously thin. Then from his own pocket Doggins took a metal hook; this unfolded into three separate hooks, forming a grappling iron. He attached it to the end of the rope and tossed it upwards. It caught between the two end spikes of the gate. After pulling it with his full weight to test it, Doggins swarmed up. A moment later, he stood on top of the gate pillar, steadying himself by holding on to the spike. Now Niall could see why he had chosen this spot. Because of the width of the pillar, the gap on either side of the spike was just wide enough to allow a lightly-built man to squeeze through.

Another rope was produced; Doggins tied this to the spike and dropped it down inside the wall. A moment later, he disappeared.

Niall went next. By curving his body upward, he achieved a foothold on top of the gate, then scrambled onto the pillar. The long rooftops of the barrack buildings lay below him in the moonlight. From this point he could also look south to the river, and to the skyscrapers of the spider city beyond. The white tower shone in the moonlight with its faint green phosphorescence, and immediately beyond it he could see the black bulk of the headquarters of the Spider Lord. Suddenly, he felt very exposed; he squeezed between the spikes and slid down the rope to the ground.

As the others joined them one by one, Niall and Doggins stood looking across the deserted parade ground towards the long, low buildings of the soldiers' quarters. There were no spider webs, and the unbroken window panes gleamed in the moonlight. Something about the place produced in Niall a curious impression of loneliness and sadness. When he spoke to Doggins, he found himself automatically lowering his voice, as if afraid to disturb the silence.

"Why do you suppose the spiders never came here?"

"Why should they? There's nothing here for them."

"So it's been like this ever since men left the earth?"

Doggins gave a crooked smile. "I hope so."

A few yards away to the left, something white gleamed at the foot of the wall. Niall went to investigate and found himself looking at a heap of bones. The skeleton had evidently been there a long time, and weather had made the skull thin and brittle.

He turned to Doggins: "Somebody tried to get in."

Doggins stirred the bones with his foot; some of them fell apart. "I'd like to know why he died there." He looked thoughtfully at the top of the wall.

"Perhaps a spider caught him."

"Perhaps." He sounded unconvinced.

A thin, high wail shocked them both; it was like the cry of some strange bird. Then Niall realised it was coming from the group at the foot of the wall. Doggins called: "What happened?"

"It's Cyprian." A man was writhing on the ground, his body arched in agony.

Doggins dropped on his knees beside him. "Cyprian, what happened?"

The man tried to speak, but the pain convulsed his lips; as he choked, a white foam appeared on his lips. Then, suddenly, he twisted backwards and stopped struggling. His eyes had turned upward, showing only the whites of the eyeballs. Doggins took his pulse, but it was already obvious he was dead. It had all taken less then ten seconds.

Doggins stood up; he looked very pale. "Anyone know what happened?"

They shook their heads; Niall could see they were stunned and close to hysteria.

Doggins raised the dead man's right arm and turned it over. On the underside of the forearm, there was a scratch about an inch long.

"That's what did it. The spikes are poisoned."

The thought of how close they had been to death sobered them all. But Doggins was determined not to allow them time to think about it.

"We've got to get moving. Now listen carefully. One of these buildings is an arsenal. I want you to find out which one it is."

Niall pointed to a building in the north-eastern corner. "I think it could be that one."

"Why?"

"It was marked on the map."

Doggins shook his head. "It looks like an office building to me. But let's find out."

Closer examination proved that he was correct. They forced the door by using their shoulders as battering rams, then lit oil lamps and spread throughout the building. Most of the rooms contained desks and filing cabinets. The air smelt stale and dead, like the air in a tomb, and dust blackened their hands whenever they touched anything. When Niall tugged on a curtain, it tore like wet paper.

Doggins was pulling out all the drawers of a desk. When one proved to be locked, he took out a knife and worked it into the crack, twisting the blade impatiently. It snapped, but Doggins gave a grunt of satisfaction as he opened the drawer. He weighed the long-barrelled gun in the palm of his hand.

"What is it?"

"A Flecknoe blaster." He took it to the window and examined it in the moonlight.

"What does it do?"

"Releases pure energy. Watch."

There was a blue flash that made Niall jump, and a thread of twisted light seemed to leap from the barrel; at the same time there was a smell of heated metal and ozone. Through the wall at the side of the window, Niall could now see moonlight. The blaster had made a neat circular hole about six inches in diameter.

"How did you know it would be there?"

"Just a guess—this isn't the first barracks I've been in." He patted the gun. "Now we're ready if we meet a spider."

"Is that what you were hoping to find?"

"One of the things."

Milo appeared in the doorway. "There's nothing here, sir. It's just an office building, as you said."

Doggins asked Niall: "Are you sure this was the location of the arsenal?"

Niall closed his eyes. He had made no special effort to memorise the layout of the barracks—it had seemed unimportant at the time—but he could still see the word "Arsenal" in the north-eastern corner of the plan.

"Yes. Quite sure."

Doggins shook his head. "In that case, the map must have been deliberately inaccurate."

"But why should it be?"

"Because in the twenty-first century, army installations were always being attacked by political terrorists. That's why they made this place so impregnable."

"But in that case, surely they would have hidden the arsenal?"

Doggins snapped his fingers. "Of course—that's the answer. Below ground." He turned to Milo. "Is there a cellar in this place?"

"Yes, but it's locked."

"Show me where it is."

Milo led them along the corridor and down a flight of stairs. At the bottom, there was a steel-covered door. When its handle refused to turn, Doggins placed the blaster against it, and fired. The door swung open, drops of molten metal cascading to the floor.

But the rooms beyond proved to be storerooms. They contained filing cabinets, boxes of papers and cassettes of microfilm. Doggins ordered everyone to examine the walls for signs of a secret door, but a long search revealed nothing.

"You've *got* to be right," Doggins said. "With a barracks in the middle of a city, they couldn't take the risk of making the armoury accessible. One terrorist bomb could blow them all off the planet. The only sensible thing would be to construct it underground." He stared with sour frustration at the floor beneath his feet.

Again, Niall closed his eyes and tried to envisage the map. He said finally:

"The word 'Arsenal' wasn't on the building itself. It was somewhere in front of it."

Only Doggins' eyes betrayed a glint of satisfaction. "Show me."

Outside, Niall pointed to the area adjacent to the building's northern wall. "About there."

Doggins turned to the others. "All right, we're looking for some kind of entrance, probably a concealed trapdoor. Spread out over there and stamp your feet. Keep on stamping until it sounds hollow."

Niall joined them as they stamped over an area of twenty square yards. The ground under their feet was smooth and black, and after ten minutes, both his feet felt sore. Doggins was crawling on his hands and knees, looking for a hairline crack; Niall could sense his increasing disappointment. The others gradually ceased their efforts.

Mostig's assistant said wearily: "Now if it was water, my old grandad could have found it in two minutes. He was the best dowser for miles."

It reminded Niall that he himself had often located underground springs; such an ability was part of the survival equipment of every desert dweller. Jomar had even claimed to be able to sense the burrows of rodents. He took the telescopic rod from his pocket and made it expand.

Doggins asked curiously: "What's that?"

He smiled. "A magic wand."

He observed with satisfaction that the metal seemed to tingle against his fingertips. Holding the two ends firmly in clenched fists, he turned his hands outward so the springy metal curved like a powerful bow. Then, forcing both hands down, so the curve was parallel to the ground, he walked forward slowly, closing his eyes to increase his concentration. When he reached the wall of the building, he turned and traced a diagonal path towards the perimeter wall. Within ten feet, the rod twisted upward with an irresistible force. Niall stopped and pointed to his feet.

"There's something down there."

Doggins said: "Bring the lights."

He and Niall both crouched on all fours and examined the hard asphalt. But the closest examination revealed no evidence of a trapdoor. Doggins asked:

"Are you sure there's something there?"

"Yes." The rod had spoken more clearly than words.

"All right." Doggins stood up. "Stand back." He pointed the blaster at the ground and pulled the trigger. The blue thread crackled like a miniature bolt of forked lightning, and the air filled with the ozone smell and with the pungent odour of burning asphalt. As they watched, the ground sagged, then dissolved. The edges of a two-foot hole bubbled and hissed, sending up plumes of white smoke. Niall joined Doggins at its rim; the ground felt hot through his sandals.

"Look at that!" Doggins gave a chuckle of delight and slapped Niall on the shoulder. "No wonder it didn't sound hollow."

From their position directly above the hole, they could see that the asphalt at this point was more than two feet thick. A lowered oil lamp showed a flight of steep concrete stairs descending into the darkness.

Doggins ordered them to fetch curtains; they returned with arms full of the mouldy and disintegrating cloth, and these were packed over the molten edges. Then Doggins was lowered into the hole, a rope tied under his armpits. Niall and Milo followed.

From below, Niall could see that the asphalt had covered a wide trapdoor whose edges were supported by curved steel buttresses, each six inches wide. He asked:

"How could anyone lift that from above? It must weigh half a ton."

"It wasn't intended to be lifted from above. The doors are controlled from below—the switch is probably in the office building." Doggins stepped carefully around the pool of tar that was slowly solidifying on the steps. "Follow me and watch out. This place may be booby trapped."

Niall said: "In that case, you'd better let me go first. I'll use this." He extended the telescopic rod in front of him.

"All right, but for God's sake be . . ."

The sentence was never finished. As Niall took his first step from the bottom of the stairway, there was a click, followed by a thud. Something flashed before his eyes and he found himself looking at a solid metal barrier which had slid across the corridor in the blink of an eyelid. It had snatched the telescopic rod from his hand and trapped it against the opposite wall. There could be no possible doubt that if it had been Niall's body that had intercepted the door, it would now be crushed flat, or perhaps divided in two as if by the stroke of some enormous axe.

Yet the sense of control engendered by the thought mirror was so powerful that Niall experienced only a mild sense of shock; his brain had already countermanded the flow of adrenalin before it had time to reach his bloodstream. As he reached out to try and pull the rod free, his hand was perfectly steady. But the rod was trapped as if in a vice.

Doggins said drily: "You see what I mean." But his face revealed how deeply shaken he felt. "Stand back."

He pointed the blaster at the edge of the door, a foot below the rod. In the blackness, the blue light made the enclosed space look like a wizard's cave; Niall observed that it caused faint sparks to crackle in Doggins' hair. As the door became red hot, then white hot, they had to move back up the stairs. A few drops of molten metal ran like drops of water, then a hole the size of a fist appeared. There was a click, then the door was no longer there. It had moved so fast that it was no more than a blur, and had vanished into the wall before the telescopic rod had reached the ground.

Niall bent to pick it up, and swore as the metal burnt his fingers. He knelt down and examined it by the light of the lamp. Incredibly, the metal was not even dented.

Once again, he extended the rod at arm's length. This time, nothing happened; whatever mechanism had triggered the release of the door had been destroyed by the heat.

Another twenty yards brought them to a heavy metal grid like a prison gate; it looked formidable, but its lock melted immediately under the heat of the blaster. Ten feet beyond this was another solid steel door with a combination lock. Doggins raised the blaster, then changed his mind. "No, let's play it safe." Niall watched with fascination as he placed his ear against the dial, then moved the knob gently back and forth with his fingertips. After ten minutes, there was a series of clicks and Doggins was able to pull the door open. It was then that they realised the wisdom of his decision not to use the blaster; stacked immediately behind the door were piles of red explosives cases, each decorated with a skull and crossbones.

These cases proved to be the final barrier. When they had been removed and restacked in the corridor, their lamps showed them a long, low-ceilinged chamber that was full of wooden cases and metal boxes. As they stood in the entrance, their lamps raised above their heads, Niall caught a glimpse of Doggins' face. His eyes were shining with the expression of a man who has achieved the goal of a lifetime.

Niall asked him curiously: "Did you know this place existed?"

Doggins started, like a man awakened from a dream. "I'd heard rumours. There were always lots of rumours. But I didn't really believe them." He drew in a deep breath. "My God, there's enough stuff here to start a war." He went forward and peered at the labels on the cases. "Rockets, firebombs, fission capsules, atom grenades . . ." He was like a man repeating some sacred litany.

Niall turned to Milo. "You'd better go and get the others." When Milo had gone, he went and joined Doggins, whose light glimmered at the far end of the storeroom. He found him sitting on an ammunition case, his hands drooping loosely between his knees.

"Are you all right?"

"Yes. Why?"

"You look ill."

Doggins shook his head slowly. "I'm not ill. Just . . . a little frightened."

"Of what?"

"Of all this power." He was staring straight in front of him. Niall sat beside him. "You realise what this represents? It's power to change the world. Power to do what you like . . ."

"To get rid of the spiders?"

"Oh yes, even that."

Niall was puzzled. "I don't understand. You've always had explosives."

"Not just explosives." He pointed. "Do you see that?"

He was pointing to a pile of black metal boxes, each about three inches thick and eighteen inches long. The label fixed to the wall above them said: "AFLs."

"What does AFL stand for?"

"Automatic fission laser." He went across to the pile and opened the topmost case. "Better known as Reapers."

"Yes. I've heard of those."

But Doggins was not listening. He was staring down into the case with a gentle, almost meditative expression. Then he reached down and brought out the weapon. To Niall, it looked disappointingly small, hardly more than a toy. It was black, little more than a foot long, with a short wooden butt and a short, heavily reinforced barrel. Below the barrel there was a curved hand grip.

Doggins brought it back to his seat and examined it slowly and carefully; he handled it as if it were a newborn baby.

Niall asked: "Haven't you ever seen one before?"

"Not in good working order."

The others were waiting inside the door. "Come here." Doggins beckoned. "I've something to show you." He allowed the weapon to swing upside down by its shoulder strap. "You wouldn't think this was the deadliest weapon ever invented, would you?"

It was obvious they had never seen a Reaper before. Milo asked: "Deadlier than the hydrogen bomb?"

"Far deadlier. Nobody dared to use the hydrogen bomb because it was too indiscriminate. This little thing could wipe out an individual or a whole army."

Niall asked: "Is it more powerful than your blaster?"

"Far more. And far more accurate. The trouble with the blaster is that the beam spreads out, so it's useless at a range of more than forty yards. This thing has a range of two miles."

Niall asked dubiously: "Isn't that too powerful?"

"No, because it's adjustable. This lever can increase or decrease its range. Set it on nought and it won't fire at all. Set it on one, and it has a range of fifty feet. And so on up

to ten. If you set it on ten when you want to knock down a
wall, you'll end up destroying half the city." He turned to
Mostig's assistant. "Ulic, I want you to hand one out to
everybody. Then I want you all to spend a few minutes
familiarising yourselves with the adjustable control. And
don't forget—never—and I mean *never*—point it at another
man unless you mean to kill him."

The word "kill" produced in Niall a curious inner
contraction, as if some cold wind had caused his heart to
shrink. It was not the word itself, but the way Doggins had
said it—as if killing were some normal and perfectly
legitimate activity.

Milo handed him a Reaper. It was surprisingly heavy for
its size—at least fourteen pounds—and most of this weight
seemed to be concentrated in the swollen cylindrical chamber immediately above the trigger guard. Its weight made it
natural to hold it with the butt pressed into the muscles
above the hip, the left hand clenched tightly around the
projection below the barrel. As he held it in this position,
Niall experienced a sensation that puzzled and disturbed
him. It was a sense of familiarity, as if he had been handling
weapons all his life.

Doggins, meanwhile, had been exploring the other aisles
of the storeroom. He had found a crowbar and was forcing
open a long wooden packing case. This proved to contain an
eight-foot metal tube and a number of bomb-like projec-
tiles. Doggins chuckled with satisfaction as he tossed one of
these up and down in his hand.

"Look at this little beauty."

"What is it?"

Doggins pointed at the tube. "That's a Brodsky Battering
Ram, and it's the greatest anti-tank weapon ever made. It's
deadly accurate up to a range of a mile." He looked fondly

at the projectile. "This thing could knock a hole in a ten-foot wall."

Suddenly, Niall knew what had disturbed him a few minutes before, It was the fact that the Reaper gave him a sensation of control and power. It was a completely negative power—since the weapon had no purpose but destruction—yet it was strangely satisfying nevertheless. The Reaper concentrated his will in exactly the same manner as the thought mirror.

Milo approached them. "What are these?" He was holding out a handful of shining metal spheres, each one hardly more than an inch in diameter.

"Fire bombs. How many are there?"

"A dozen cases."

"Good. Make sure everybody fills his pockets with them. Then get ready to leave. It's time we got out of here." He replaced the lid on the packing case.

Niall said: "Do you mind if I ask you a question?"

"Go ahead."

"When we set out this evening, were you hoping to find Reapers?"

"Of course."

"Then what made you change your mind?"

"About what?"

"About fighting the spiders."

Doggins shook his head. "Let's get one thing clear. I don't intend to fight the spiders." He hefted the Reaper in his hand. "This isn't for fighting. It's for bargaining."

"About what?"

"Freedom."

"But I thought . . ."

Doggins interrupted him. "Freedom from interference. Why do you suppose we use oil lamps instead of electric torches? Why do you think I light the damn things with a tinder box instead of matches? Because of the spiders."

"I didn't think they had any control over the beetles."

"It's in the Peace Treaty: 'No servant of the beetles shall be allowed to use or construct a machine.' So no dynamos, no engines, no computers—not even a clock. And it's been like that for more than two hundred years."

"And what would they do if you broke the agreement?"

"Go to war, I suppose. And this time they'd make sure they destroyed us."

"Could they destroy you?"

"Easily. When they made the treaty, there were about the same number of beetles as spiders. Now the spiders outnumber beetles by a thousand to one." He grinned and patted the Reaper. "But with this thing, we outnumber the spiders by a thousand to one."

Milo approached and saluted. "We're all ready, sir."

"Right. Take them up on the barrack square and wait for me."

Niall asked: "What would happen if the spiders found this place?"

"It wouldn't matter. They wouldn't be able to get in."

"You shouldn't underestimate Kazak."

"I don't." They had reached the door. "Help me move these boxes."

Together, Niall and Doggins stacked the red explosives cases inside the door where they had found them. When the last one was in place, Doggins closed the massive door and twisted the dial of the combination lock. Then he struck the dial with the crowbar until it lay smashed on the floor.

"There. Even Kazak shouldn't be able to open that. And if he does, he may regret it."

As they mounted the concrete steps, Doggins stopped and placed his hand on Niall's arm.

"There's something I want to say to you."

"Yes?"

"Just—thanks for helping me to find this place. Perhaps I'll be able to do you a good turn one of these days."

Niall smiled. "You already have."

OUTSIDE IT WAS UNEXPECTEDLY DARK. The wind had risen and a black raincloud obscured the moon. The tiny flames of the oil lamps only seemed to increase the surrounding blackness. Doggins cursed under his breath.

"I don't like this. It means the spiders can see us and we can't see them."

"Then let's wait until daylight."

Doggins shook his head; Niall could sense his indecision. "I don't want to stay here a minute longer than I have to."

Someone asked: "What are we going to do with poor Cyprian?"

"We'll have to leave him where he is."

"Couldn't we find somewhere to bury him?"

Doggins shrugged. "All right. Bring him with us."

Four of them picked up the body, two holding the arms and two the legs. Doggins led them to the rear gate. He took the blaster from his pocket.

"I want to show you something. Watch."

He pointed the blaster at the centre of the metal door and pulled the trigger. As the thread of blue lightning flickered from the barrel, the air filled with the smell of heated metal; the gate turned red, then white hot. But, to Niall's surprise, it showed no sign of melting. Doggins lowered the blaster.

"It's a special blaster-proof metal called lattrix—designed to stop terrorists. The wall's made of a similar material. Now watch."

He adjusted the lever on the Reaper, then pointed it at the gate. The thin blue beam that emerged from the barrel was like an illuminated glass rod. Where it struck the gate, a small hole appeared in the metal. Casually, Doggins raised the Reaper; it made a tiny blue flame as it burnt and left a thin, straight line behind it. Within a few seconds, Doggins had sliced a large section out of the gate; it fell outward with a dull crash that emphasised its weight. Niall could see that the metal was six inches thick.

Doggins said: "Put the lamps out and follow me. Keep your guns at the ready, but don't fire unless I give the order."

He led the way. As Niall passed through the aperture in the gate, he ran his finger over the metal; it was cold to the touch.

The others had stopped. Niall assumed they were taking their bearings until he heard the soft thud; it was unmistakably the sound of a body being dropped. Then, as he stepped clear of the gate, the paralysis struck him and held him frozen in mid-stride. As the moon emerged from behind the cloud, he saw the spiders who were waiting for them. They were standing on the opposite side of the road, and they looked like black statues. The moonlight was reflected from their blank eyes.

This time Niall experienced no fear. He even observed that although the paralysis affected his muscles—so that his arms felt dead as though their circulation had been cut off by a tourniquet—his eyes were still able to move normally, and his brain was totally unaffected. Moreover, since the thought mirror was still turned inward, he was able to intensify his concentration, bringing the familiar sense of focused power. As he did this, the paralysis in his arms and shoulders began to melt away; if he relaxed the concentration, it returned. It was a curiously satisfying sensation, like pushing back a tide of impotence. A more powerful effort pushed back the tide towards his feet, so that his whole body was free. It was clear that the spiders were totally unaware of what was happening.

Then one of the spiders moved towards them and he decided it was time to act. He raised the Reaper and pulled the trigger. Nothing happened, and he realised that the lever was still in the safety position. He pushed it forward with his thumb and pulled the trigger.

The spider disappeared. So did the railings behind it, and a large section of the façade of the building. The blue pencil of light was dazzling in its intensity, and the weapon made a distinct recoil against the muscles of his stomach. When he released the trigger, his eyes were still dazzled by the flash. The momentary silence seemed frightening and unnatural.

The other spiders—there were perhaps six of them—were still immobile, but now it was the immobility of shock. And as Niall turned the Reaper on them, he was already aware that it was unnecessary. Their will force had snapped at the moment the first spider disappeared. It was as if they were connected and the destruction of one affected all. This is why, although he pointed the weapon towards them, he made no attempt to pull the trigger. Their helplessness somehow disarmed him.

As he hesitated, another beam lanced through the darkness and struck the nearest spider, then travelled sideways, cutting them down before they could move. The effect was at once fascinating and sickening. The beam sliced them in half, like some immense knife, at the same time cutting through the railings behind them. A moment later, the smell of burning flesh filled the air. The top half of a spider's body rolled into the gutter, while the legs and the lower part of its belly collapsed on to the pavement. There was no convulsive twitching, nothing to indicate death by violence. The bodies looked as though they had never been alive. All this had taken place so swiftly that it seemed instantaneous.

Doggins lowered the Reaper. He nodded at the weapon in Niall's hands. "You turned it up too high."

"I know." The lever was on five.

"But thanks all the same."

It was a signal for the others to surround him; some tried to hug him, some shook his hand, others patted him on the back until he winced. Their gratitude was overwhelming, both emotionally and physically—a measure of the terror it had replaced. None of them had ever experienced paralysis of the will, and the experience had shaken them more than the death of their comrades. Niall could understand this; it seemed a denial of the most basic human assumption: of control over the body. The experience was like a premonition of death.

"All right," Doggins said, "that's enough. We've got to move." He was adjusting the lever on his gun. As he pressed the trigger, Niall closed his eyes involuntarily. When he opened them, the remains of the spiders had vanished; in their place, there was a shallow crater in the pavement. Niall asked:

"Wouldn't it be better to take shelter in the Fortress until daylight?"

"Yes, but not in the Fortress. That's the first place they'll search. We'll find a basement somewhere." He turned to Milo. "Do you still want to bring Cyprian?"

Milo hesitated. "Whatever you say."

Doggins pointed his Reaper at the corpse, then seemed to change his mind.

"Bring him along. We'll try and hide him until we can get back."

As they lifted the body, a few drops of rain fell on the pavement. In the windy blackness they could not even see one another; so they stumbled on in a chaotic group, frequently colliding but deriving a certain comfort from the physical contact. When a blast of cold wind indicated that they had reached a street corner, Doggins asked Niall: "Any idea where we are?"

"The town hall is over there."

"All right. We'll make for that."

A glimmer of moonlight revealed a street running in a northerly direction. It was wide, and its buildings looked relatively undamaged. Because there were no cobwebs overhead, they marched in the middle of the road. But the weight of the corpse slowed their progress. After they had travelled only half a block, Doggins said: "Stop here. Put him down. I'm going to see if I can find a basement."

They waited in the darkness, shivering in the wind that flowed past them like an icy current. A few moments later, there was a yellow flicker of light from below the level of the pavement. This was followed by the blue flash of the blaster. Then Doggins' voice called: "All right. Bring him down here."

He was waiting at the bottom of a flight of steps that led into the basement area. Behind him, a door stood open. As they entered, the rain began to fall in torrents. A gust of wind caught the open door and slammed it behind them.

The lamp revealed that they were in a large furnished

room. The floor was carpeted, and there were tables, armchairs and a glass-fronted bookcase. Even Niall could tell that this had once been a comfortable flat. Now it smelt of dust, mould and decaying plaster. Yet the sound of the rain on the pavement, and the wind that shook the windows, induced in them all a sense of relief and comfort.

The window curtains were of a heavy, stiff material, and—unlike those in the barracks— untorn and undecayed. When these had been drawn, Doggins allowed them to light all the lamps. A heavy chair was lifted against the door to prevent it from blowing open—the Reaper had destroyed its lock. Then they attempted to make themselves comfortable and settled down to wait for the dawn.

All looked strained and exhausted, and Niall could see that some were close to breaking point. Only a few hours ago, they had been full of euphoria, amused and exhilarated at the thought of defying the authority of the spiders. Now three of their number were dead, and the rest were aware that they might never see their homes again. Yet none of them showed resentment; none seemed to blame Doggins for leading them into this grim situation. As he looked at their pale, tired faces, Niall felt admiration as well as pity.

It was when one of them took an apple from his pocket and began to eat that Niall remembered the food tablets; he produced the box from his pocket.

"Is anyone hungry?" They all looked up hopefully, but their faces fell as they saw the tiny brown capsules. Nevertheless, each took one; even Doggins, who at first waved them away impatiently, was induced to swallow one. Niall chewed his own, and within minutes experienced the wave of pleasure and relief as the warmth coursed down his throat, then slowly expanded until his stomach was filled with the comforting sensation of a hot meal. On the others, the effect was immediate. The air of listlessness vanished as the colour returned to their cheeks; suddenly, they were talking as animatedly as if the past few hours had been a dream.

Doggins asked: "Where did you get these?"

"From a machine."

Doggins gave him an odd look, but said nothing.

The rest of the flat proved to consist of a kitchen and two bedrooms. The kitchen walls were covered with black mould, and the red floor tiles were half-buried in plaster that had fallen from the ceiling. But the bedrooms were surprisingly dry, and in these they found blankets, eiderdowns and pillows. They were intrigued by the clothes they found in the wardrobes, and some of them proceeded to try them on. There seemed to be a general agreement that the male garments of these ancient times—particularly the trousers— were funny as well as ugly, while the female dresses were altogether more practical.

Ulic discovered a wall cabinet full of bottles and glasses. Doggins' eyes gleamed as he examined a bottle of amber liquid.

"Scotch whisky. It's an old drink like wine. I once found a bottle in a sunken wreck." He peeled off the leadfoil from the neck, removed the cork and sniffed it. Then, to their alarm, he raised it to his lips. All watched with concern, expecting him to collapse or spit it out; instead, he grunted with approval, and took a longer drink. He handed the bottle to Niall. "Try it."

Niall found the taste startling and disagreeable, completely unlike the golden liquid he had shared with Odina on the ship. But a few minutes later he realised that the effect was much the same: the soothing, glowing sensation, and the expanding euphoria. As he watched the others pouring the fiery liquid into glasses, he experienced a flood of emotion that startled him. It was as if they were participat-

ing in some religious ceremony, or some ritual of blood-
brotherhood. It lasted only for a few moments, but during
that time achieved a remarkable intensity. For the first time
in his life, Niall was overwhelmed by a feeling of love for
his fellow men, and for the human race as a species. These
young men whose names he scarcely knew—Ulic, Milo,
Yorg, Crispin, Hastur, Renfred, Kosmin—had suddenly
become as dear to him as his own mother or brother.

As the heat of the oil lamps and of their bodies gradually
increased the temperature, the room became pleasantly
warm. It was then that they all became aware of an
unpleasant smell: that of decaying meat. Niall, who had
smelt it before, realised after a moment that it came from
the body that lay stretched out in the corner. The face had
turned purple, and the ankles and wrists were beginning to
swell. The scratch on the underside of the forearm had
become a gaping black wound, and this seemed to be the
source of most of the stench. Cyprian's body was dragged
into the kitchen and left under the table. As an afterthought,
Niall covered it over with the plastic tablecloth. As a mark
of respect, Milo insisted on leaving one of the lamps
burning on a chair beside the body. Cyprian had been his
cousin.

Suddenly, they were all tired. Niall tried to look through
the books in the bookcase but his eyes refused to focus. It
had been twenty-four hours since he had last slept. He
settled into an armchair, pulled a blanket around his shoulders, and surrendered to the fatigue. The voices around him
seemed to be filtered through some dense, stifling medium,
yet they still aroused a sense of warmth and kinship. This
feeling of contentment carried him like a wave into a
dreamless sleep.

He woke up with a curious sense of discomfort, as if
something sticky was pressed against his face. As he raised

his hands to try and push it away, it seemed to dissolve. The room was now illuminated by a single lamp, and everyone was asleep. For a moment the silence worried him; then he realised that the wind had dropped and the rain was no longer beating on the windows. In the next armchair, Doggins was snoring softly. At his feet, a black haired youth named Kosmin was sleeping on his back, his mouth wide open. He seemed to be having some kind of nightmare and kept gasping uncomfortably.

Then Niall became aware of the sound. It was very soft and difficult to define: a bubbling, liquid noise, with an element like the rustling of dry leaves. For some reason, Niall associated it with the suffocating sensation that had awakened him. At first it seemed to be coming from the other side of the front door, and he imagined it to be connected with rainwater; then he became aware that it was coming from the kitchen. When he tried to move, a pain shot through his skull and he realised that he had fallen asleep with the thought mirror turned inward. He reached inside his shirt and turned it over; the sense of relief was instantaneous.

He stood up cautiously, allowing the blanket to drop to the floor, and took the lamp from the table; then, stepping over recumbent forms, he made his way to the kitchen.

What he saw made him gasp and take a step backward. The space underneath the table seemed to be a seething mass of grey slime, heaving like the scum on top of a bubbling cauldron. When he stooped and held the lamp closer, he realised what had happened. A squid fungus had made its way through a hole in the ceiling, and was now consuming the corpse. Niall picked up a broom that was lying on the floor, and poked the bubbling mass; it ignored him.

A voice whispered: "What is it?" Doggins had been

awakened by his movements. When he saw the fungus, he recoiled with disgust. After watching it for a few moments, he shrugged. "Oh well, perhaps it's the best thing that could happen."

"Is there any way of killing it?"

"Fire or the blaster. Otherwise it's almost impossible."

"What would happen if you cut it in half?"

"Nothing much." Doggins produced the broken knife, and slashed at a writhing grey tentacle. It fell to the floor, where it wriggled like a worm. Niall watched with horrified astonishment as the main body of the fungus seemed to spread sideways like a viscous liquid, while at the same time, the writhing fragment moved towards the fungus. They joined, and the fragment was absorbed by invisible mouths.

"Are they dangerous?"

"Only if you can't get away. Otherwise they move too slowly to do much harm."

"But what do they feed on most of the time?"

"No one's sure. They seem to be able to live for years without food." Doggins yawned and went back to his chair.

For another five minutes, Niall continued to watch the fungus with a mixture of fascination and disgust. It was diffusing a smell of rotting vegetation, and its thousand tiny mouths made a continuous liquid noise as it devoured the body. A trail of slime, running from the hole in the ceiling and down the kitchen wall, revealed that the creature had the ability to cling to smooth surfaces. It seemed to eat at an extraordinary speed; through the heaving slime, the outline of Cyprian's body had already ceased to be distinguishable.

As disgust gave way to curiosity, he deliberately focused the process of inner-contraction until his inner being was as still as water on a windless day. For a moment, he shared the predatory consciousness of the fungus, its total absorption in the process of digestion, and was interested to realise that the creature was aware of his presence. It could sense him as a diffused mass of life-force, a potential meal and a potential danger. But while it was eating, Niall was unimportant. Then his awareness slipped beyond the low-grade consciousness of the fungus, and once more became aware of the rippling, pulsating energy that seemed to spread through the earth like wavelets on a pond. Suddenly, he knew beyond all shadow of doubt that the life of the squid fungus was in some way dependent upon this energy source. It was difficult to grasp the precise nature of this dependence. At first he was tempted to believe that the fungus had no life of its own, but received life direct from the energy-pulse; but this was obviously absurd. A more accurate way of putting it might have been to say that the fungus was "subsidised" by the energy-pulse as a tree is subsidised by the living soil. This would explain how the fungus could live in empty buildings for years without dying of starvation . . .

Niall's hair prickled, and a feeling of excitement drenched him as if someone had emptied a bucket of icy water over his head. The insight that surged through his mind was vague and half-formed, yet he felt it to be of tremendous significance. Not a tree, but a plant . . . This creature was a kind of mobile plant. It was now feeding on this corpse exactly as the roots of a plant feed on decaying organisms in the soil.

But the energy-pulse was trying to raise this mass of fungoid vegetation to a higher level; it was trying to turn it into a kind of animal. This was part of the insight that filled Niall with such excitement. It was the recognition that although this creature possessed no intelligence, it was nevertheless being driven and controlled by a force that possessed intelligence. This recognition filled him with a feeling of delight mixed with vague alarm, but also with a consuming curiosity to understand more about the mysterious pulse. Could it, for example, sense his own presence?

He went back into the other room, stepping carefully across recumbent bodies.

"Could I borrow your blaster?"

Doggins, who was still wide awake, asked: "What for?"

"I want to try something."

Doggins pulled it from his pocket. "Be careful. It's getting low, but it could still set the place on fire."

Niall returned to the kitchen. He knelt down, pointing the blaster at the edge of the slimy mass, and pulled the trigger. The blue lightning filled the air with the smell of ozone. A six-inch area of the fungus turned into black charcoal. The rest of the fungus shuddered and contracted with alarm. And as this happened, the pulse itself faltered. Then the grey protoplasm withdrew from the carbonised area, leaving it stuck to the floor. The creature went on feeding as if nothing had happened. It lacked the intelligence to flee.

Yet it had told Niall what he wanted to know. As the blast had struck it, Niall had been able to sense a momentary interruption of the pulse, revealing that it was aware of the attack. There was a two-way relation between the fungus and the energy-source.

Five minutes later, the fungus ceased to feed. Moving very slowly, it slid from under the table with a contractile motion, not unlike a slug, and reared up against the wall. Nothing remained of Cyprian's body; on the slime-covered tiles, there were only a few buttons and other indigestible objects. Niall pointed the blaster at the creature, tempted to destroy it; only the thought of the smell deterred him. It seemed to sense his intention and moved up the wall with surprising swiftness; a few moments later, it had disappeared through the hole in the ceiling.

Idly, merely in order to observe the effect, Niall concentrated his will and ordered the creature to stop moving. Although it was now invisible, he could sense its presence. He could also sense its reluctance to obey. Its one desire was to retreat to some dark, damp corner and digest the food it had absorbed so efficiently. Using the thought mirror to direct and concentrate his will, Niall ordered it to return. It started to do so, and a grey tentacle appeared around the edge of the hole. And at that point, the energy-pulse intervened, and countermanded Niall's order; the tentacle withdrew. Now thoroughly intrigued, Niall concentrated his inner-force and again ordered it to return. For a moment, a kind of tug of war ensued. Then the energy-source seemed to give way. The reason, Niall was convinced, was that it sensed that nothing important was at issue. The fungus wriggled through the hole, and started to cross the ceiling.

Niall had lost interest, and he relaxed his will. He expected the creature to stop, then to retreat. Instead, it continued to wriggle across the ceiling, then down the wall. Puzzled, he continued to watch its progress. It reached the floor, then flowed across the tiles, brushing aside chunks of fallen plaster, and reached his feet. He pointed the blaster, prepared to destroy it if it made any attempt to attack. But it merely waited there, an enormous, pulsating mass of semi-vegetable, semi-liquid greyness, waiting for further orders. With astonishment, Niall realised that it had come to accept him as the source of its instructions. Suddenly, the temptation to destroy it had disappeared. Instead, Niall ordered it to return. Once again, he relaxed his will as soon as he had given the order. But the fungus retreated obediently up the wall and vanished through its hole.

Now the kitchen was empty, it seemed pointless to leave the lamp burning. Niall leaned over, cupped one hand over the bulb-like chimney and blew it out. A grey light filtered through the dusty window pane, and when he peered upward past the railings he could see the first rays of sunlight striking the clouds above the eastern rooftops. With a contraction of alarm, he realised that the lamp had been visible from the street. He stood there for perhaps five minutes, staring up into the greyness; then, seeing no sign of movement, went back into the other room. Doggins was the only one awake. He accepted the blaster without comment and pushed it back into his pocket.

Niall said: "It will soon be daylight."

"Thank God for that." Doggins stretched and yawned, then clapped his hands. "All right, boys, time to get up. With luck we'll be home for breakfast." He went to the nearest window and peered through the curtains. "We'll get started in ten minutes."

They woke with sighs and yawns, but all became instantly alert when they remembered where they were.

Milo went to the kitchen and a moment later called out: "Cyprian has gone!"

Doggins said irritably: "We already know that. We'll talk about it later. Get ready to leave."

But Milo's words had introduced a sense of foreboding, and it hung over them as they stood up and rubbed the sleep out of their eyes. They had lost their eagerness to venture out into the dawn.

Doggins said: "Now before we set out, I want to say something, and I want you all to listen as if your lives depended on it. Now listen." He held up the Reaper. "This weapon is more than a match for any spider. With this in your hands, you could defy an army of spiders. But remember that it's just as dangerous to human beings as to spiders. One false move, and you've killed the man standing in front of you—or, worse still, sliced off his arm or leg. So if we're attacked, don't panic. Keep your nerve, and don't pull the trigger until you can see your way clear. Don't take *any* risks.

"Now there's one more thing I want to say. You may be afraid that a spider can paralyse your will before you can pull the trigger. So I want to tell you something that I've been keeping to myself. I realised a long time ago that this will-power of the spiders isn't as irresistible as we think. In fact it's a mistake to call it will-power. It's more like a force of *suggestion*." It was obvious that they were puzzled and doubtful. Doggins smiled reassuringly. "Look, why do you obey me when I give you an order? I don't force you to obey it, do I? You do it because you've come to accept the idea that I give the orders. Suppose somebody came up behind you and shouted in your ear 'Stand up straight!' You'd probably obey—but not because of his will-power. You'd obey because you've been taught to obey orders. Now I'll tell you what I believe. I believe that when a spider paralyses your will, it sends out a kind of beam of suggestion, and the beam affects your subconscious mind. You could say it's a kind of hypnotism, if you know what that means. But you can refuse to be hypnotised. And with one of these things in your hands, you've got a damn good reason for refusing.

"So next time a spider tries to paralyse your will, don't let it get away with it. Fight back. Tell yourself there's nothing to be afraid of.

"All right, that's enough. When that door is open, I'll go first. Follow me one by one. Niall, you come last. Set your weapons to one, but don't fire unless I give the order. Crispin, move that chair out of the way. Then Milo open the door."

Niall said: "Wait . . ."

Because his mind was still open to the vibrations of the energy-pulse, he sensed what was about to happen even as the fair-haired youth took a step towards the chair. It was like the breath of wind that signals the coming of a hurricane. Instinctively, he contracted his will as if tensing to receive a blow. So when the paralysis struck a moment later, like a chain of freezing metal, his own mind was already clenched like a fist. In that brief moment of preparation, he knew that Doggins was right. The will-force of the spiders was like an order suddenly bellowed into the depths of the mind. But although his muscles felt as though he had been plunged into freezing water, his will remained unaffected. When he reached up to push forward the safety catch of the Reaper, his fingers felt numb and frozen, yet they obeyed his will.

The door was being pushed open with such force that the heavy armchair began to move even though it was wedged under the handle. Niall waited calmly, his finger curled round the trigger. But a movement made him glance sideways. Doggins' face seemed to be distorted with agony, and his lips were drawn back from his clenched teeth. He looked like a man struggling to raise some enormous weight. Then his arm jerked, and blue flame leapt from the muzzle of his gun, sliced through the back of the armchair and penetrated the door. A moment later, Niall also fired into the widening gap.

Instantly, the will-force snapped, leaving them free. Niall darted forward and pushed the chair back against the door; it encountered no resistance. The others were staggering drunkenly and some stumbled or fell to the floor. Doggins turned and grinned at them.

"All rights, lads, round one to us." But his voice was strained and breathless. "Remember what I said: don't lose your nerve." His face suddenly became grey and he took a step backwards and sat down heavily.

Niall asked: "Are you all right?"

Doggins nodded. "I'm fine. Give me five minutes and I'll be ready to go."

Niall asked incredulously: "You're going out there?"

"Of course. We can't stay here all day." He closed his eyes and leaned his head back. The beaky nose gave the sallow face a corpse-like appearance.

For the next five minutes no one spoke. They were all watching the door, their weapons at the ready, and Niall was struck by the fact that no one looked tense or anxious. In this situation of extreme danger, there was no room for doubts or misgivings.

They were startled into alertness by a creaking sound; it was unmistakably the gate in the area railings. A moment later, they heard the noise of feet descending the steps. No one moved. There was a knock on the door, and a voice called:

"May I come in?"

Niall said: "It's Kazak."

Doggins called: "Are you alone?"

"Yes."

Doggins called to Ulic, who dragged aside the armchair and opened the door. Outside, it was daylight. Kazak bowed and smiled as he came into the room.

"I am King Kazak." He regarded Niall with a kind of ironical affection. "Yes, I thought I'd find you here." Doggins had risen to his feet. "And you must be Mr. Doggins. May I sit down?"

Someone hastened to push forward a chair. It was plain that Kazak's dignity, and his obvious lack of fear, had made an immediate impression on the young men. He sat down carefully and deliberately. Doggins also sat. Kazak said:

"I am here as an emissary of the spiders. I've come to bring you their offer. They have asked me to say that you are all free to go."

His words caused astonishment. Doggins said incredulously: "You mean we can go back home?"

"That is correct, but on one condition—that you hand over all your weapons."

Doggins shook his head vigorously: "Never."

Kazak seemed mildly surprised. "May I ask why?"

Doggins grinned. "Because I don't trust them. We'd never get out of this place alive."

Kazak shook his head. "You are mistaken." He said it with total conviction, and Niall could see that he was sincere. "If you handed over your weapons, the spiders would come to an agreement with the bombardier beetles. Once that had happened, it would be a question of keeping their word. Your safety would be guaranteed. They have no wish to go to war."

Niall said: "If we handed over our weapons, they wouldn't need to go to war. They could destroy us whenever they liked."

Kazak nodded. "Possibly. But I am quite certain that they would keep their promise."

Doggins asked: "How can you be certain?"

"Because I am certain that the spiders want peace."

Doggins shook his head. "I'm afraid the answer has to be no."

It was obvious that Kazak was not surprised by this reply. He considered it carefully for a moment, frowning at the floor.

He asked finally, "So you intend to destroy the spiders?"

"No. We want peace."

"They have offered you peace."

"But on their terms. They might change their minds when we've surrendered."

"I believe you are wrong." Again, Niall could see that he was sincere. "But in any case, let me try another suggestion. Suppose we could reach an agreement to destroy these weapons, so that neither side possessed them. Would you agreed to that?"

Doggins thought about this for a long time, then shook his head, as Niall had known he would. "No."

"May I ask why not?"

"Because while we have these things we have bargaining power. They cost the lives of three of our men. Why should we throw that away?"

"They have also cost the lives of seven spiders." Niall was surprised that he knew the precise number. "Why not let one debt wipe out another?"

Doggins said patiently: "For a very simple reason. At the moment, you're a slave and I'm a slave. With these things, we needn't be slaves any more."

"I do not feel myself to be a slave." The contraction of Kazak's forehead showed that the notion offended him.

Doggins shook his head stubbornly: "Yet you are, just as I'm a slave of the beetles."

Kazak's neck flushed. "Are the spiders any worse than the beetles?"

"Much worse." It was Niall who answered. "When I first came to the spider city, I talked to your nephew Massig. He is quite convinced that he has nothing to fear from the spiders. He thinks he'll spend the next twenty years of his life working for them, then be allowed to retire to the great happy place. Even the slaves believe they're perfectly safe. When I first came to the slave quarter, I saw a child throw something at a spider in its web. I expected to see him killed instantly. Instead, the spider rolled him over on the ground and everybody thought it was a marvellous joke. It wasn't until last night that I realised what's really happening. The slaves are kept on the move all the time—they're not even allowed to sleep in the same place for two nights running.

So when a slave gets eaten, nobody notices. Massig knew all about the slaves being eaten, but it didn't worry him because he was quite sure *he* was safe."

Kazak listened politely, but the tightness of his lips betrayed his impatience. "All that I know."

"Yet you still trust the spiders?"

Kazak shrugged. "For the moment, I have no alternative. They are the masters. What message do you wish me to take back to them—that *you* wish to be the masters?"

Doggins said: "Not masters. Just equals."

Kazak nodded thoughtfully: "Perhaps even that could be arranged."

Doggins smiled broadly. "If you can do that, you've got yourself a deal."

Kazak stood up. "Let me go and see what can be done." He moved towards the door, and Ulic and Milo pushed the chair aside. At the door, Kazak turned to face them again.

"Would you be willing to give up even one of your weapons? Merely as a token of good faith?"

Doggins patted the Reaper. "Not one of these, I'm afraid. They could blast us all out of this place before we could bat an eyelid."

"Have you nothing you could offer me as a bargaining counter? Something I could show them as a symbol of your good faith?"

Doggins took the blaster from his pocket.

"How about this?"

"Very well." Kazak took it from him by the barrel and dropped it into the pocket of his toga. "I will return in a few minutes."

When the door had closed behind him, Niall asked: "Was that a good idea?"

Doggins shrugged, smiling. "I don't see why not. Those things are peashooters compared to these. Anyway, it's running out of power. I noticed that when I used it to blast the lock. It won't last much longer."

The youth called Kosmin asked: "May I ask a question?"

"Of course."

Kosmin said awkwardly: "I'm not questioning your judgement, but would it be such a bad idea to accept their offer?"

Milo said: "I was going to ask the same thing."

Kosmin said: "Suppose we agreed to destroy the Reapers, and they reached a diplomatic agreement with the beetles—wouldn't that be good for everyone?"

Another said: "While we're got these weapons, they won't stop trying to destroy us."

Doggins nodded. "That's true, Hastur. But while we have these weapons, we have the power to destroy them. As soon as we hand them over—or allowed them to be destroyed—we are at their mercy."

Milo said: "But do you think we can get out of here alive unless we make some concessions?"

Doggins said: "Yes, I do. For two reasons. The first is that we're stronger than they are. The second is that they know it. That's why they sent Kazak to bargain with us. We'd be stupid to throw away that advantage."

Niall said: "They could have had another reason."

Doggins looked at him curiously. "Such as?"

"To gain time."

Before Doggins could reply, there was a knock on the door and Kazak's voice called: "May I come in?"

Milo pushed the chair aside, and Kazak came past him. This time he stood near the door. Niall thought he showed signs of uneasiness. He cleared his throat and began:

"First of all, the spiders have begged me to try again. They emphasise that they only wish for peace. They would even be willing for you to return to the city of the beetles with your weapons, providing you will promise to destroy them when you are there." He went on quickly as Doggins started to speak. "You see, they don't seem to trust human beings. I don't mean they doubt your word. But they don't believe there can be any permanent peace while you are armed with Reapers. They believe that men have a curiously criminal or destructive streak, and that sooner or later, the weapons would be turned against the spiders. As a human being, I must confess that I'm inclined to agree. Aren't you?" He looked around at all of them as he spoke, and Niall could see that most of the young men were nodding. Kazak undoubtedly had a way with words.

But Doggins shook his head decisively. "I'm sorry, Kazak. There's no way in which we're going to agree to part with the Reapers. If they won't allow us to leave freely, then we shall be forced to shoot our way out. And if necessary, we could annihilate ten thousand spiders—and I mean literally annihilate."

Kazak sighed. "In that case, you force me to deliver the second part of the message—and I can assure you that I hate it as much as you will. I am merely the messenger." He looked squarely at Doggins, and at Niall, who was standing beside him. "They have asked me to point out that they are holding Niall's mother and brother as hostages . . ." He paused, and Niall could sense his nervousness. "They also ask me to tell you that they have now captured the city of the bombardier beetles, and that all your families are also hostages. If you hand over your weapons, or agree to their destruction, they will all be freed. Moreover, Niall's mother and brother, and anyone else he wants, will be allowed to move to the city of the beetles." He lowered his eyes. "That is my message."

Doggins had gone red, and veins stood out on his

forehead. "If those bastards harm a single one of our people, I swear I'll destroy every spider in this city."

His eyes were so fierce that Kazak looked away. He cleared his throat. "I can only repeat what I say. They have no intention of harming anyone. They only wish for peace. They will exchange the lives of your families for the Reapers."

Niall glanced at Doggins. From his look of bafflement and helpless fury, he could see that Doggins felt he had no alternative.

Niall touched his arm. "This is something we need to discuss."

Kazak smiled with relief. "Please take all the time you like. Would you like me to withdraw?"

Niall said quickly: "Yes, perhaps that might be best."

Kazak bowed gravely, smiled his thanks at Milo for opening the door, and backed out. No one spoke until his footsteps reached street level. In the silence, Niall could sense their shock and dismay.

Doggins said in a flat voice: "Well, I'm afraid that's it."

But Niall had already turned the thought mirror so it faced inward, and the sudden concentration had dissipated his own sense of defeat.

"You intend to surrender?"

Doggins shrugged. "Can you see any alternative?"

"Yes. To refuse."

"How can we take that risk? They wouldn't hesitate to kill our families."

Niall looked round at the others; he could see they all shared this opinion. He said:

"Listen to me. My own family is also being held hostage, so I understand your feelings. But what good would it do to surrender? You don't trust the spiders. Try to put yourself in the place of the Spider Lord. You have defied him once.

You might do so again. The only way to prevent that from happening is to destroy you and your families. Do you think they would hesitate if you placed yourself in their power?"

He could see that his words had filled them with dejection and foreboding and went on quickly. "But suppose you refuse to surrender. It is true that they may carry out their threat against your families. But if they do, they know you would never rest until you have taken the life of a hundred spiders for every human being. While you have the weapons, you are in a position of power, and they can only take that away by destroying you. Why throw yourself on their mercy? You are only inviting them to kill you as well." He turned to Doggins. "And how do you know they are telling the truth? Is the city of the beetles undefended?"

"Of course not. But it could be captured—especially if they launched a surprise attack."

"And would that be easy?"

Doggins smiled grimly. "No. The beetles don't trust the spiders."

"So the spiders may be trying to trick you into handing over your weapons?"

Doggins thought about this, frowning at the floor. He looked at the others. "What do you think?"

This appeal obviously embarrassed them; they were used to being given orders.

Milo said hesitantly: "I think Niall may be right."

Doggins came to a decision. "Open the door. Take the chair away."

Daylight streamed in. For a moment they were all dazzled. Doggins strode to the doorway. "Kazak, can you hear me?"

Kazak's voice shouted: "Yes."

"Tell them we're coming out." He turned to the others. "Keep your weapons ready, but don't fire unless I give the order. And keep a watch about your heads—don't forget they can drop out of the sky."

He advanced into the daylight and mounted the steps. The others followed in a single file; all held their weapons at the ready. As he mounted the steps, Niall glanced upward. There was now a cobweb that stretched across the street between the rooftops, but he could see no sign of an ambush.

As he stepped out of the gate, Niall was shocked to realise how many spiders were waiting for them. There must have been ten thousand, packed closely together in both directions, to the corners of the street and beyond. The only empty space in the road was immediately in front of the area gate. The spiders had withdrawn in a wide semi-circle; the nearest were standing with Kazak on the far side of the road. Yet to Niall, even this distance brought an almost uncontrollable sense of being trapped. With a shock, he realised that spiders regard human beings with as much dislike as men regard spiders or poisonous snakes. They saw him as a disgusting, pale-skinned, venomous creature who threatened their lives, and every one of them would have been delighted to plunge its fangs into his throat. Once again, he experienced a sense of physical coldness as their blank eyes stared at him.

Niall could see that the others were badly unnerved. In an effort to prevent his hands from shaking, Milo was holding his weapon so tightly that his knuckles were white. Kosmin looked as if he was about to be sick. Doggins was very pale, his face beaded with sweat. The wall of sheer hostility seemed to drain their vitality. Even with the thought mirror turned inward, Niall felt that his own control was on the point of dissolution. Black patches were drifting across his vision.

Kazak called: "Well, have you decided to accept our terms?"

His voice restored Niall to a sense of normality; the feeling of suffocation suddenly vanished. He stepped forward in front of the others and answered firmly: "I'm afraid the answer is no."

Kazak was obviously surprised. He asked gravely: "Don't you think that is a rash decision?"

"No." Suddenly, Niall knew that the time for words had passed, that this deadlock could only be broken by some form of action. He pointed. "Do you see that building?" He turned his weapon on the ten-story building on the south-eastern corner of the street and raised it so that it pointed above the heads of the spiders. Then he pulled the trigger.

What happened shocked him, even though he had been expecting it. The gun recoiled so it almost jerked itself out of his hands, and the blinding flash of blue energy struck the building and seemed to turn it into a dazzling blue haze. The recoil swung the barrel through an angle of a few degrees, and even this slight movement was enough to tear a fifty-foot hole in the wall. With incredulity, Niall realised that the blast had cut through the building as if it were made of paper; he could see the blue sky through its far wall. Then the whole building sagged and collapsed, showering slabs of masonry down on to the street.

Niall had released the trigger almost immediately, appalled at the magnitude of the catastrophe he had unleashed, but the collapse continued as if the building had been devastated by some tremendous explosion. A vast section of wall fell directly into the street below and onto the massed ranks of spiders. At the same moment, the spiders facing them surged forward, as the agony of dying spiders battered them like some tidal wave. Niall was aware that their minds had been momentarily destroyed by horror; but his companions, who had no way of realising this, opened fire. Their Reapers, set at a lower level than Niall's, acted like flame throwers, cutting pathways through the massed bodies of the spiders and filling the air with a sickening stench of burnt spider flesh. Then, suddenly, they were surrounded by fleeing spiders, none of whom made any effort to attack them. All control had vanished. The agony, communicated from mind to mind, had destroyed the living as much as the dead.

Only Niall could understand what had happened. For the others, it was a baffling miracle. They had braced themselves for destruction, and now their enemies had vanished. But for Niall, the defeat of the spiders had left behind a nausea that was spiritual, not physical, in origin.

Something moved in the gutter on the far side of the road. It was Kazak. He stood up slowly, then came across the road towards them, his steps as unsteady as those of a drunken man. His toga was torn, and both knees were gashed and bleeding. So was his face; a flap of skin hung loosely under his left eye, which was already beginning to turn black. He stopped in front of Niall, and asked in a thick voice:

"Was that necessary?"

Niall tried to speak, but his voice seemed to be trapped in his throat. It was Doggins who answered.

"Well, it seems to have done the trick." He wiped his dripping forehead. "I didn't think we were going to get out of that alive."

Niall found his voice. "I'm sorry, I didn't intend that to happen. I only wanted to show them how powerful these things are." He was surprised by the waves of calm that were now flooding over him.

Doggins laughed. "You certainly succeeded." He turned to Kazak. "Well, are you going to stick with us?"

Kazak looked like a tired animal; the blood was now running down his cheek. He stared at Doggins for a long time, and it was difficult to guess what was going on in his mind. He said finally "No," then turned and limped slowly away from them, moving in the direction of the river.

Doggins obviously found his decision incomprehensible.

"Is he cunning, or just stupid?" he asked Niall.

But Niall was also baffled. He stared after the limping figure with an odd feeling of concern.

"I don't know."

Doggins shrugged cheerfully. "Oh, well, it doesn't matter one way or the other." He turned to the others. "Are you lads ready to go?"

THEY MARCHED IN A NORTHERLY DIRECTION, advancing down the centre of the wide street to avoid the risk of a surprise attack. All felt instinctively that this was unlikely; but it would have been foolish to relax their precautions. Doggins used his Reaper to slice through the webs that stretched overhead, and their strands hung like festive streamers down the walls of the buildings, fluttering in the still breeze from the south.

At the far end of the street, they found themselves at the edge of the town hall square. The City Hall was a massive pseudo-Greek building with fluted columns that had long ago turned black, but the surrounding lawns were smooth and well kept. Although the square was totally deserted, they paused to survey it, wondering if they were being observed from the buildings around or from the City Hall itself.

Doggins said: "I don't like this. Surely they can't be

stupid enough to let us march straight out of their city without any attempt to stop us?"

The same thought had occurred to Niall. The spiders were badly demoralised. Yet the Spider Lord must know that if he allowed them to escape now, he would have lost a major opportunity—perhaps the only opportunity—to destroy them. Surrounded by buildings, Niall and his companions would be vulnerable to a sudden rush. And at close quarters, the spiders were almost irresistible. Once they had paralysed their victim, even for a moment, by sheer will-power, they could despatch him instantly with their poisoned fangs.

Niall was staring thoughtfully at the City Hall. "Do you know anything about spider balloons?"

"Of course. Our people manufacture them."

Niall pointed. "That place is a silk factory. Perhaps they also store balloons there."

Doggins frowned, shaking his head. "That's no good. We'd also need porifids."

"Porifids?"

"Short for Porifera Mephitis, the things that make them fly. Also known as the skunk-sponge. It's a kind of sponge that produces a lighter-than-air gas."

"But if there are balloons, there may be porifids too."

Doggins glanced at the sun to calculate the time. "All right. I suppose it's worth a try."

They approached the City Hall cautiously, their weapons raised; but there seemed no sign of life. In the beds outside, banks of coloured flowers filled the air with a spring-like fragrance. Birds sang in the surrounding trees, which rustled in the cool breeze. Niall was interested to observe how danger sharpened his appreciation of these things.

The carved oak doors were locked, but yielded immediately to the thin beam of the Reaper. Inside was a large hallway with marble columns and two wide flights of stairs sweeping in a curve to the upper storey. It was not unlike Kazak's palace, but larger.

Facing them was another pair of imposing wooden doors, which also proved to be locked. Doggins sliced out the lock with his Reaper and kicked open the door. He gave a chortle of delight, and flung his arm round Niall's neck.

"You're a brilliant little lad! How did you know?"

The hall that faced them had evidently been used once for public ceremonies; the walls were covered with banners bearing municipal emblems; now it was a workshop and storeroom, full of ladders, wooden planks, handcarts, and building materials. And in the far corner were piles of neatly-folded silk which Niall recognised as spider balloons.

Niall shrugged modestly. "It was just a guess."

Doggins turned to the others. "You lads spread out all over the building and stand guard at the windows. We can't risk a surprise attack. Wedge the front doors closed. If you see any sign of movement, let me know immediately." He turned back to Niall. "Let's see if we can find a skunk sponge."

"Where are they usually kept?"

"In some kind of a tank."

In an alcove behind the balloons, they found a locked door; when this was kicked open, they were met by a stench of rotting vegetation that made them both recoil. Holding his nose, Doggins peeped into the room. He nodded with satisfaction.

"That's what we need."

There was a large glass tank, its sides almost as high as a man, containing slimy green water. Propped beside it were a number of nets with long handles. Niall peered into the scummy liquid but could see very little. Doggins climbed a flight of wooden steps beside the tank, took one of the nets and fished about in the water.

"There we are." He held out the net. Lying in the bottom, among slimy weed, was a green pulsating object shaped like a doughnut. The hole in its centre was closed, but when Doggins prodded with his finger it opened for a moment, then closed on his finger. Inside this mouth Niall caught a glimpse of a pointed green tongue. Doggins pulled his finger away with a faint plop. The air was immediately filled with the disgusting smell of decay.

"But how does it make the balloons fly?"

"I'll show you."

Doggins crossed to a cylindrical metal container that stood on a table in a corner. When he removed the lid, a stench of rotting meat mingled with the vegetation smell. Doggins picked up a rusty saucepan from the table and dipped it into the cylinder. When it emerged, it was half-full of big grubs, some of them as much as two inches long and thick as a finger. Still holding his nose and retching with digust, Doggins tilted the saucepan over the creature shaped like a doughnut. The mouth promptly opened, and closed again hungrily on the wriggling grubs. Once more the air filled with the smell of decay.

Doggins put the saucepan down. "Ugh! Let's get out of here." As they left the room, he carefully closed the door behind him. Niall observed that other porifids were now swimming at the edge of the tank, obviously hoping for grubs.

Back in the hall, they lifted down one of the folded balloons and laid it out on a clear floor-space. Unfolded, it was thirty feet across. This was the first time Niall had seen a spider balloon at close quarters, and he examined it with curiosity. He had often wondered how the spider was supported; now he could see there was a kind of flat, silken bag underneath the balloon. This had room for a large body and could easily hold two or three human beings.

The balloon itself was not spherical, but flattened like two dinner plates held face to face, and the finely woven silk was slightly sticky to the touch.

Spread out on the floor, the balloon formed a huge blue-white disc on the edge of which there was a six-inch loop of rope held in place by a powerful clip. When this was released and pulled, the side of the balloon opened like a gutted fish. Niall, who was barely familiar with the principal of the slide fastener, found this remarkable. Inside the balloon, at its central point, there was a reinforced cup about a foot in diameter, covered with two broad straps.

Doggins pointed. "That's where the porifid goes."

"But how do you make it produce the gas?"

"You don't have to. They hate the darkness, so as soon as they're sealed in, they begin to produce gas."

"And how do you release it?"

"Through a valve in the undercarriage. Help me get this thing outside."

Large windows behind a speaker's rostrum revealed a courtyard in the centre of the building. They dragged the balloon outside and spread it on the flagstones. Doggins then fetched the fishing net and emptied the porifid into the cup-like container, enclosing it with the straps—since the creature seemed to have no power of locomotion, these were obviously intended to prevent it from falling out rather than from escaping. The balloon was then closed and sealed with the slide fastener. Even as this happened, it began to swell. Doggins found a coil of rope and secured the balloon to a metal ring in the flagstones. While he was doing so, it began to float clear of the ground. Half a minute later, it was fully distended and floating sideways at the end of a taut rope some twenty feet above their heads. Niall tried pulling on the rope, but the balloon seemed to actively resist any attempt to drag it towards the ground. He chuckled.

"How are we supposed to get inside it?"

"I'll show you."

Doggins placed his hands on his hips and stared up at the balloon, wearing a frown of intense concentration. His face became red, and a vein began to throb in the middle of his forehead. For about a minute, nothing happened; then the balloon began to deflate and drifted down towards them. Doggins expelled his breath in a long gasp and wiped the perspiration from his face.

"It's hard work. But I'm told it gets easier once you've got used to it. You can make them re-absorb their own gas. That's how the spiders control them." The balloon was already reinflating and rising again.

They heard running footsteps in the hall; a moment later, Milo came into the courtyard.

"There's something happening out there, sir."

In the entrance hall Ulic and Hastur were looking out the windows, their weapons at the ready. The lawns surrounding the building were still deserted; so was the large paved area of terrace in front of them. But on the pavements on the edge of the square, there was a continual movement of spiders and human beings.

From the top of the staircase, Renfred called: "They're all around the edge of the square. You can get a better view from the roof."

They followed him up to the third storey and out through a door on to the flat roof. From this vantage point there was an excellent view of the whole square. It revealed that all the surrounding streets were full of spiders and human beings. Yet there was no sign of any attempt to advance towards them; the square itself remained deserted.

Doggins frowned. "I wish I knew what they're up to. I daresay they mean to try and rush us."

Renfred was looking nervous. "I suppose we shall have to shoot our way out?"

Doggins shook his head. "We're leaving by balloon. Hastur, Milo, collect the others and bring them into the courtyard. Renfred, you wait there and keep watch—don't hesitate to open fire on full power if they attack."

Niall said: "I think I'd better stay and keep watch." Renfred would be an easy victim if the spiders launched a sudden attack.

"All right. We'll send for you as soon as we're ready to leave."

Alone on the roof, Niall used the thought mirror to concentrate his perceptions. The apparently aimless movement of spiders and human beings worried him. He tried to put himself into the place of the Spider Lord. If he wanted to prevent a group of dangerous enemies from escaping, how would he go about it? The simplest method would be a sudden rush. A spider could move at a terrifying speed; those who were now five hundred yards away could be swarming all over the City Hall within twenty seconds. But if they intended such an attack, why were they not massing in ranks on the pavements at the edge of the square?

He tried to relax and attune his mind to what was happening, but found it difficult. There were too many spiders, and all seemed preoccupied with their own affairs. He was expecting to sense an atmosphere of hostility, a determination to destroy their human enemies; instead, the spiders seemed to be waiting for something. But for what? An order to attack? That seemed unlikely; there was no sense of immediate expectation.

Niall strolled to the inner edge of the roof and looked down into the courtyard. They were bringing out balloons one by one and piling them on top of one another. Doggins was talking earnestly to a small group that included Milo and Kosmin, obviously explaining the steering mechanism of the balloons. The inflated balloon was floating within a few feet of Niall's face, its skin taut. The porifid inside was evidently producing large quantities of gas. It was leaking from some escape valve, and the stench of putrid vegetation drifted towards him; Niall moved hastily upwind.

As he watched, Ulic brought out another porifid in its net; this was sealed into the balloon at the top of the pile. A few moments later, the balloon began inflating. Milo, Kosmin and Hastur clambered quickly into the undercarriage, and Doggins once more pointed out the position of the release valve. The undercarriage was made for the large, flat body of a spider, not for upright human beings, and its three occupants slid into uncomfortable positions in which their bodies reclined at an angle of forty-five degrees, while their feet met in the centre. Horizontal slits served as windows, allowing them to look out. The balloon was already rising into the air, and those who were trying to hold it down had to let go. A moment later, it shot past Niall, pushing the other balloon aside. Niall caught Hastur's eye and thought he looked at once terrified and exalted. Then the balloon rose above the roof and was caught by the strong breeze. It continued to shoot upward with alarming speed, and within thirty seconds was a mere dot against the clear blue of the northern sky.

All movement at the edge of the square had ceased; spiders and human beings were all staring upward. Niall tightened his grip on the Reaper. If there was going to be a sudden attack, it should happen now, as the spiders realised their enemies were escaping. But as the balloon turned into a dot and then vanished, the movement of the spiders resumed. Again, Niall tried hard to attune himself to their minds, but found it impossible; there was too much confusion and activity. But again he received the impression that they were waiting for something.

Five minutes later, a second balloon went up. Once again, the movement among the spiders ceased. This time, Niall felt he could detect a certain tension; but it vanished as the balloon receded out of sight. But when a third, and then a fourth balloon rose up from the courtyard, he could sense a change. As they saw their enemies escaping, the spiders were becoming impatient. The aimless movement had ceased, and he once more experienced the curious sense of physical coldness that told him he was the object of scrutiny. In spite of the warmness of the morning, his arms were covered in goose-pimples as if he were standing in a cold wind.

Doggins looked up at him; the fifth balloon was already inflating. "Come on down. We'll be ready to go in a moment."

But Niall experienced a curious reluctance to leave his post. He preferred to stay where he could see the spiders.

"I'd better wait until the other two have gone."

Doggins shrugged; he obviously felt Niall was being overcautious.

As the fifth balloon rose clear of the roof, the feeling of coldness seemed to increase. He began to experience the sense of nausea that he had felt half an hour before, when he was surrounded by spiders. It had the curious effect of blurring his vision and making the sweat stand out on his forehead, although it felt as cold as rain. He became aware that this was not due to a deliberately-directed hostility, but simply to the feeling of loathing of which he was the object. He had to take long, deep breaths to keep his senses clear.

The sixth balloon shot past him, making him start with

alarm. Now there was only Doggins in the courtyard. "Come on down now," he called. "We're ready."

Niall cast a final glance round the square, then hurried through the door that led down off the roof. At that moment, the feeling of oppression vanished so abruptly that he felt as if some physical load had been lifted from his head. Then, as he passed a window on the stairs, he understood the reason. The square had turned into a black mass of spiders, all racing towards the building. The first of them were already crossing the surrounding lawns. He ran down the stairs three at a time, but as he reached the hallway, the double doors shuddered under the impact of a heavy body. He raised his weapon and started to press the trigger, then saw that the door had been wedged with a heavy baulk of timber and that it would take a battering ram to burst through. He ran across the storeroom and out into the courtyard.

"Quick. We're being attacked."

As he spoke, there was a sound of shattering glass from the hallway. Doggins began to scramble into the undercarriage of the balloon which was hovering four feet above the ground. Niall slammed the courtyard door behind him and heaved a large stone flower vase against it, astonished by his own strength. Then, helped by Doggins, he climbed into the undercarriage, sliding head-downward. As he scrambled into an upright position, he felt the balloon beginning to rise. At the same moment, the first of the spiders arrived at the edge of the roof surrounding the courtyard. It leapt, and they heard its soft impact on the top of the balloon. Doggins was sawing at the rope that held them, but its slackness made it difficult to cut. Then Niall became aware that, instead of ascending, the balloon was returning towards the flagstones. Doggins cursed and struck with his clenched fist above his head, where a damp patch indicated the presence of the porifid. The effect was instantaneous; there was a violent upward surge and the frayed rope parted with a jerk. Another spider launched itself from the roof, struck the balloon and plunged onto the flagstones below. Then the roof was below them, and they could see the swarming black bodies of the spiders. A gust of wind tilted the balloon, and a spider hurtled past them, legs flailing, and plunged towards the roof. It struck the edge of the parapet, bounced off on to the lawn below and lay still. Both of them began to laugh uncontrollably; if the under-carriage had felt less unstable, they would have flung their arms round each other.

In less than a minute, the City Hall was only one building among many. They could see the barracks and the river, and beyond that, the main square with the white tower and the headquarters of the Spider Lord. And in the barrack yard, Niall saw something that made his heart contract: a crowd of men and of spiders gathered in the corner where the armoury was situated.

The balloon could be controlled by two ropes that were attached to fin-like rudders on the underside. Now, as the red spires of the beetle city appeared in the distance, Doggins began to steer a course towards it. He also tugged on the cord of the release valve and for a moment they were sickened by the overpowering stench of decay. As the fabric of the balloon became less taut, it began to descend.

Niall was staring back towards the city, thrilled by this panoramic view which reminded him of his vision in the tower and filled him with an absurd sense of being lighter than air. In the distance, beyond the hills on the southern edge of the city, the sea was glittering in the sunlight like a clouded mirror. To the east, there was a wild countryside of dense woodland, with mountains on the horizon.

Then his attention was drawn back to the city they had

just left. There was an orange flash, followed by the thunder of an explosion; he could see clearly that it came from the barracks. A black cloud of smoke began to rise into the air, carrying with it large fragments of solid material. As he shouted to Doggins and pointed there was a second and far greater explosion which was followed by a whole series of smaller explosions; these seemed to be spread over a far larger area than the barracks. As the noise roared in their ears, the wind struck them like a blow and sent them spinning through the sky. They were hurled up, and then down, and Niall caught a glimpse of the earth up above his head. With sudden terror he realised he was on the roof of the balloon, the naked sky above him and the undercarriage collapsed around him. Doggins was thrashing wildly in an attempt to escape the enveloping folds of silk, and Niall saw stars as he was kicked on the side of the head. Another blast of wind struck them and again the balloon was sent spinning, Niall clinging frantically to the loose silk. As his grip began to slacken and he felt himself slipping off the edge, the balloon performed a somersault and he found himself once more in the safety of the undercarriage. The Reaper was sticking into his back, and Doggins was lying across his chest and suffocating him with his weight. Niall twisted away from under him and managed to turn over on to his knees. The balloon was still tossing like a ship in a storm, and the sounds of explosions continued to roll past them like volleys of thunder. Finally, Niall succeeded in separating himself from Doggins and standing upright.

What he saw shocked him. It looked as if the whole city had disappeared. Instead, there was a billowing black cloud of dust and smoke which seemed to be moving upward and sideways in slow motion, like sand disturbed at the bottom of a river. Niall's first thought was of his family. Then, as some of the smoke drifted aside, he saw with relief that the explosion had been confined to the slave quarter; he could clearly see the white tower and the headquarters of the Spider Lord behind the expanding clouds.

Doggins pulled himself up beside him. "My God, that was a close one." He was obviously shaken; his knuckles were white as he clung to the fabric of the undercarriage. As he stared at the heaving smoke, his expression changed to one of awe. He drew a deep breath.

"Well, that's the last you'll see of your friend Kazak."

"Kazak?" For a moment Niall failed to understand. "What makes you think he was responsible?"

Doggins grinned with malicious amusement. "It was Kazak all right. He tried to get into the armoury with my blaster."

Niall shuddered as he realised how close they had been to destruction. "So that's what they were waiting for!"

Doggins turned away. "The treacherous bastard got what he deserved." He shook his head. "But what a waste of explosive!"

They were both so fascinated by the spreading black cloud that neither had paid any attention to the land immediately below. Now, suddenly, Doggins gave a cry of alarm and pulled violently on the cord of the release valve; the stench hissed past them and was whipped away by the wind. The balloon gave a shudder and began to descend. They were almost directly over the twisted spires of the beetle city. And all round the city, staining the green landscape like a black mildew, was an army of spiders.

Doggins began to laugh. Niall stared at him in surprise, then realised that he was laughing with sheer relief, and was, in fact, close to tears. Doggins placed a hand on his shoulder.

"You were right. They *were* bluffing. They haven't captured the city."

"Can you be sure?" Niall was still suspicious of a trap.

"Look." Niall followed the direction of his pointing finger. At first he was not sure what Doggins was trying to indicate. He seemed to be pointing at the main square, with its expanse of green lawn. Then Niall observed a movement and realised that the lawn was covered with a densely-packed mass of green-backed beetles—so many that the paths were no longer visible.

"But why are they all there? Why aren't they defending the town?"

"They are."

"I don't understand . . ."

But Doggins was no longer listening. He was staring below, and at the same time thumping the balloon above his head with his clenched fist. When Niall looked down he understood why. Instead of descending at an angle towards the city, they were plummeting almost directly downward, on a course that would take them into the midst of the spiders. At the same time, the sense of physical coldness told him what was happening. The combined will of the spiders was being directed at the porifid inside the balloon, causing it to re-absorb its gas so that the half-filled balloon was falling like a stone.

Doggins said between his teeth: "Right, if that's what you want." He unslung the Reaper from his back and pushed its lever forward. Then he braced himself against the side of the undercarriage and pointed the weapon downward.

In the bright sunlight, the beam of energy was almost invisible. But as it struck the ground, blue flame seethed in all directions like a sea of blue fire. Spiders shrivelled and vanished and the earth became black. Then, suddenly, black bodies were fleeing, colliding and scrambling over one another in their terror. Niall was fascinated to observe that those who ran towards the beetle city were suddenly halted, as if they had crashed into an invisible wall. Then, almost immediately, they struggled to their feet and fled in another direction. He was witnessing the same mass panic he had seen earlier that morning—a panic in which the instant communication of physical agony produced a mindless terror and total loss of control.

Once again the balloon was struck by a force like a hurricane. This time it was the heat blast rising from the ground like the updraught of some immense bonfire. Niall was flung to his knees, and for a moment the heat was so intense that he was afraid the fabric would begin to burn. The undercarriage swung wildly from side to side as the balloon was hurled upwards. When he stood up and looked over the side, the ground was again receding fast.

Doggins shouted: "I'll steer, you release the gas." He handed Niall the cord of the release valve. For the next five minutes, Doggins performed a miracle of control, sometimes apparently steering the balloon directly into the wind. Niall held the cord but made no attempt to use it; it was simpler to control the porifid by will power. The creature seemed to be remarkably sensitive to mental commands, releasing and reabsorbing gas with a precision that made it possible to achieve total control of the vertical component of their descent. At one point, when the wind almost carried them into one of the twisted spires, Niall caused the balloon to rise so that it missed the top by a few inches.

By now, people were running below them, trying to keep up with the balloon. In the forefront of the crowd, Niall recognised Doggins' wife Selima. The balloon caught momentarily in the branches of a tall tree, brushed the wall of a house and finally touched down beside an ornamental pool. Hands reached out to grasp theirs and to help them out of the collapsing undercarriage. Selima threw her arms round Doggins' neck and kissed him repeatedly. Niall found himself surrounded by people who were asking questions, while a young girl placed a coloured paper chain round his neck. A small boy was clinging to his hand and asking if he could have a ride in the balloon. Further confusion ensued as the balloon started to rise again; but when Doggins pulled the slide fastener that released the pressure, there were cries of disgust and one child was violently sick. Niall held his breath until he had moved upwind from the stench.

He had been scanning the faces, hoping to see Odina, but there was no sign of her. For a moment, the sight of a blonde head made his heart pound; then he realised it was Doggins' wife Lucretia. He pushed his way towards her.

"Where is Odina?"

"Odina?" For a moment she did not seem to understand him. "Oh, she's with the beetles."

"Is there something the matter?" Her face looked drawn and tired.

She gave him a strange sidelong glance. "What do you think?" She pushed her away towards her husband, brushed Selima impatiently aside, and whispered something in his ear. Doggins' smile suddenly vanished and was replaced by a look of anxiety. With some difficulty, Niall reached his side.

"What is it?"

"Trouble."

"Spiders?"

Doggins gave a twisted smile. "Far worse than that. I've been summoned before the council."

"But why?"

Doggins shrugged. "Causing trouble, I suppose."

"Shall I come with you?"

Lucretia interposed sharply: "The Master sent for you alone."

Doggins grimaced. "Not allowed. You go back with Lucretia. I'll see you later." He turned and strode off in the direction of the town hall. Selima looked as if she was about to run after him, but a glance from Lucretia checked her.

Niall turned to Lucretia and was met by a hard stare. He asked: "Can you tell me what's wrong?"

"Wrong?" She raised her eyebrows with mild sarcasm. "Oh, nothing's wrong. You've just started a war, that's all."

Selima touched his arm gently. "Come back with us now. You must be tired."

Lucretia gave a snort of irritation, and walked off.

Niall said: "I don't understand. He's saved your lives."

She gave him a sad smile. "That is for the Master to decide."

Her submission irritated him.

"But don't you feel proud of him? He's saved your city from the spiders."

"Perhaps that is true. But yesterday we had no quarrel with the spiders."

Neither of them spoke as they crossed the green lawns and turned down the smooth marble road that led to the town hall. Then the sight of a collapsed balloon by the side of the road reminded him of the others.

"How many more balloons have landed?"

"Two. But we saw another one pass overhead."

Now they had reached the town hall square. But its wide lawn was no longer crowded with beetles. As they were crossing it, a woman rushed up to Niall and seized his arm.

"Can you tell me what has happened to my son Yorg?"

"He escaped in a balloon. If he is not among those who landed, then he has been carried beyond the city. He should be quite safe."

Another woman approached him. "And my son Marcus?"

Niall lowered his eyes from her face. "I am sorry. He is dead."

The woman collapsed on the ground and began to moan and wail, beating her forehead on the hard turf. Niall felt convulsed by misery and guilt. The other woman asked:

"How was he killed?"

"He was . . . he was killed by a spider." He was about to say "eaten," but stopped himself in time.

A small crowd had gathered round them. Selima said: "He cannot answer more questions now. We have to go back."

But at that moment a beetle came down the steps of the town hall and hurried across to them. It reached out with its long front leg and touched Niall on the shoulder, then made a series of gestures with its feelers. Selima said:

"He is saying that you must go with him. They want to speak to you."

Niall stared at the blank face with its goggle eyes. It was not unlike the face of a spider, yet conveyed no feeling of menace. In spite of their enormous size, and the obvious strength in their armoured legs, the beetles somehow communicated an atmosphere of gentleness and good nature. Without hesitation, Niall followed it back into the town hall.

It took several moments for his eyes to become accustomed to the dim light. Then he saw that the entrance hall was full of beetles and that they were communicating in their peculiar, sibilant voices, which sounded not unlike the chirping of a cicada. A moment later, to his joy, he saw Odina sitting on a bench in a corner. He rushed across to her and seized her hands.

"Are you all right?"

She raised her eyes to his face; to his astonishment, she seemed not to recognise him.

"Don't you know me?"

"Yes." Her lips scarcely moved.

"Then what is it?" The emptiness of her gaze chilled him.

The beetle touched him on the shoulder. Odina looked as if she was about to speak, then shook her head. Niall turned away and followed his escort feeling saddened and shaken. He cast a glance back towards her but she was no longer visible among the beetles.

He was led down a curved, sloping ramp that led into a basement; the light here was even dimmer than in the upper part of the building. The walls were of rough, unsmoothed stone, and as he followed his guide down a long, sloping corridor, he felt as though he was entering some kind of underworld. The floor under his feet was also rough, and he had to walk carefully to avoid stumbling. Yet he could understand intuitively why this lower part of the building had been left in an apparently unfinished state. For beetles the earth is a place of refuge and safety. So it would be natural to construct a council chamber—a place demanding deep thought and calm deliberation—under the ground.

The tunnel turned a right angle, and the slope became even steeper; now the walls were of hard-packed earth, supported by unplaned wooden beams. Like Kazak's underground city, this corridor was lighted by oil lamps set in alcoves. They came to a place where the walls opened out and where the corridor appeared to come to an end; in fact, the earth wall that faced them was a massive door made of some fibrous material like peat. As they waited, it swung slowly open. Niall expected to find himself confronted by some insect guardian of the threshold, and was surprised and amused to see that it was Doggins who was struggling to pull open the heavy door, which was more than a foot thick. Doggins gave him a brief nod of recognition; Niall thought he looked grim and rather harassed. When they were inside, Niall's beetle escort closed the door with a single powerful thrust of its front legs.

They were in a large, dimly-lighted room whose floor was a shallow oval bowl. The walls were of earth, supported by pillars of undressed stone; the light came from flickering oil lamps set close to the ceiling. The oval space contained a number of protuberances, like small hillocks, and on each of these sat a bombardier beetle. As his eyes became accustomed to the poor light, Niall could see that each of these hillocks had a steeply sloping upper surface, so the beetles were able to rest on them in an upright position, each folded leg resting in a groove; it was the beetle equivalent of an armchair, designed so its occupant could peer over the raised back.

There were, he counted, fifteen beetles facing him in a semi-oval. Their blank faces reminded him of toads. The beetle at the centre of the arc was obviously older than the others, and its horny skin looked cracked and mottled. One of its goggling black eyes was flecked with white. Yet Niall sensed immediately that this was the Master.

Doggins took his arm and led him to the central point of the arc. They stood side by side. Niall was glad of Doggins' moral support. The gaze of the beetles produced in him a peculiar and uncomfortable sensation. It was completely unlike the physical coldness produced by the spiders, which seemed to be some physical expression of hostility. Yet he felt, nevertheless, as if their eyes were penetrating the surface of his skin and seeing into his body. They gave him the impression that they were ignoring his physical appearance and somehow looking directly into his feelings and emotions. It was an uncomfortable sensation, like being naked. He felt that it would be pointless to try to lie or deceive; they would sense the lie even before he spoke.

The beetle sitting to the right of the ruler raised its feelers and made rapid signs.

"Saarleb asks how old you are," Doggins interpreted.

Niall replied: "I am not sure. Perhaps some seventeen summers."

The beetle on the other side of the ruler asked a question, which Doggins translated as: "Saarleb asks why did you come to this country?" Saarleb was clearly a title, not a name.

Niall replied: "I was taken prisoner. My father was killed by the spiders."

When Doggins translated this reply, there was a long pause; then a beetle to his right asked:

"Do you want revenge on the spider who killed your father?"

Niall answered truthfully: "No."

Another beetle asked: "Do you want revenge on all spiders?"

Niall thought about this before he answered: "I do not want revenge. But I want to be free."

There was another silence. Then, for the first time, the Master spoke:

"If the spiders would allow you to leave in peace, would you be contented?"

"No."

"Why not?"

Niall was thinking of how to phrase his reply when, to his astonishment, he heard Doggins repeating the question and realised that the Master had addressed him directly. It was quite unlike the sensation he had experienced when the Spider Lord or the Steegmaster had addressed him telepathically; in that case he had experienced the voice inside his

chest or his head. But the Master had seemed to address him
as if speaking aloud.

Niall looked into the blank, worn face and answered:
"Because even in my own country, we are not free. We
have to spend our lives hiding from the spiders."

As Doggins started to translate his reply, the Master made
a sign to him to be silent. Doggins looked surprised. Then,
once again, Niall picked up the thought of the Master as
naturally as if they were holding a normal conversation.

"If your people were permitted to live unhindered, would
you be content?"

This time, the Master made no accompanying gestures,
and it was obvious from Doggins' baffled expression that he
could hear nothing. Niall thought for a long time before he
answered:

"No. I have seen the way the spiders treat their servants
and their slaves, and I regard them as my enemies. I could
not be happy in my own land."

These words caused a buzz of conversation to break out
among the beetles; they began addressing one another in
their strange sibilant language and waving their feelers.
Only the Master continued to look at Niall with his
mask-like face. Niall glanced sideways at Doggins and saw
immediately that he was worried.

It was several minutes before silence was restored. Then
the Master said:

"What you have said places us in a difficult position. We
have no quarrel with the spiders. Can you give us any
reason why we should not hand you over to them?"

Niall made an intense effort of concentration, using the
thought mirror to clarify his intuitions. He was aware that
the Master was not asking him to excuse or justify himself;
he was not asking for argument or persuasion. Behind his
question lay his own objective assessment of the situation.

They wanted peace with the spiders, and the key to peace was to hand Niall over to the Spider Lord. They were asking Niall, in an equally objective spirit, whether he did not agree that this was the most sensible thing to do. And suddenly, Niall understood what form his reply should take. He stared at the floor and placed his hands behind him in an attempt to clarify his thoughts. It was vital not to lose the thread.

"My people were once lords of the earth. Now we are either servants or fugitives. That is perhaps as it should be: we lost our position through weakness. Many of our people are content to be servants, and that is also as it should be; it is their own choice. But I was also offered a position as a servant of the spiders and I knew that it was impossible. And that is not simply because the spiders killed my father." He looked up, and stared directly at the Master. "It is because I have no wish to be a servant. My strongest desire is to be free."

The Master interrupted: "But you are free. To be alive is to be free."

Niall shook his head. "That may be true for beetles and spiders, but it is not true for human beings. We seem to have a kind of . . . of freedom function." He could sense the bewilderment of the Beetle Lord. "It is a feeling that our minds can be free as well as our bodies." He was feeling confused by their lack of understanding, and found it difficult to explain what he meant. He finished lamely: "For human beings, it is not true that to be alive is to be free."

There was a long silence. Finally, the Master said: "What you have just said is either very profound or very stupid. I do not profess to understand it. I am free. You are free. There is no other kind of freedom."

Niall asked: "Do you mean I am free to go now?"

"No. That is still for us to decide. We must consult with

the Spider Lord." He beckoned to the beetle who was
guarding the door. "Fetch the Spider Lord."

Niall was struck dumb with astonishment, and felt the
muscles of his scalp contracting. Niall glanced at Doggins
as the beetle went out and was puzzled that he showed no
sign of surprise; Doggins was staring at the floor and looked
only nervous and depressed.

With an immense effort, Niall controlled the pounding of
his heart, but could still feel the blood throbbing in his toes
and finger-ends. The minutes seemed to drag by. It seemed
to him that his last hope had gone. If the beetles had
permitted the Spider Lord to enter their city, then they were
anxious for peace at any price, and it was merely a matter
of time before they acceded to his demands.

The door opened. Niall experienced a wave of surprise
and relief when the guard stood aside to permit Odina to
enter the room. But as she came closer, he saw she was
wearing the same stunned, blank expression that he had
seen in the entrance hall. Her eyes met his without recognition; she looked as if she was in a trance. She came and
stood beside him, standing to attention like a soldier. As
Niall glanced sideways at her bare breasts and sunburnt
arms, he experienced a flood of misery, the sense of having
lost her.

The Master made a sign to the guard. "Bring the Death
Lord a seat."

"I prefer to stand."

Niall stared at Odina with amazement. The voice had
issued from her lips; yet it was the distinctive voice of the
Spider Lord. At the same time, Odina's face changed. It
had become older and stronger, the face of a stern old
woman.

The Master spoke in the strange, hissing language of the

beetles; yet Niall could understand the words as clearly as before.

"Greetings again to the Death Lord."

"Greetings." The voice was impatient.

"We have spoken to our servant Bildo, and he confirms what you have told us." It took Niall a moment to realise that Bildo referred to Doggins. "He agrees that he entered your city without permission. But he claims that his only purpose was to find explosives."

The Spider Lord said: "A servant has no business to do things without permission."

"He points out that he had been promoted to the rank of Saarleb only that afternoon, and that therefore he had the right to make that decision. But that, of course, is no excuse. He should have raised the matter in council first. And the council would have refused permission."

"Does it give him the right to kill spiders?"

"Of course not. That is the law. No human creature is permitted to raise his hand against a beetle or any of their allies."

The Death Lord said: "And the penalty for breaking that law?"

"Death."

"Do you propose to carry out that penalty?"

"If you insist, yes."

Niall glanced at Doggins; he was looking at the floor, his face emotionless.

"Will you carry it out yourself, or will you hand him over to us?"

The Master said: "We will hand him over to you."

"That is as it should be." The Death Lord was obviously mollified. "And what of the other prisoner?"

The Master hesitated. "That is a more difficult case. He

is not a servant but a prisoner. Therefore he has every right to try to escape."

"Has he also the right to kill spiders?"

"He points out that the spiders killed his father, and that he regards them as his enemies. That seems to me a reasonable attitude."

"But he *is* an enemy of the spiders. And you are our ally. Therefore it is your duty to hand him over to us."

"I agree with you. But there seems to be some doubt among my council members. They point out that we only have a non-aggression treaty. That does not involve us in your quarrels."

"That is an unfriendly attitude."

"It is neither friendly nor unfriendly. We only wish to do what is right according to the law."

"So you propose to let him go?" The Death Lord was beginning to lose his temper, and Niall was interested in this sign of weakness; it was evidence of vulnerability.

"We have not yet decided. The council has expressed a wish to hear what you have to say on the matter."

There was a long silence. Then the Death Lord said:

"Very well. If what I have to say carries any weight, I advise you to listen to me very carefully."

"We shall always be willing to do that."

"Good." The Death Lord was obviously impatient of interruption. "Then listen. You know, as we do, that these human creatures were once the masters of the earth. That was because my ancestors and yours were small enough to be ignored. But we also know that they spent all their times quarrelling and killing one another. They were incapable of living in peace. Finally, the gods grew tired of them, and made us the masters. And ever since then, the earth has been at peace.

"You beetles have treated your servants with indulgence,

and this was the cause of the quarrel between us. That quarrel ended in the Great Treaty, under which you agreed that your servants should never be allowed to gain their independence. Ever since then, you and I have been allies. Is that not true?"

"It is true." The Master spoke as if making a ritual response.

"Good." The Death Lord was obviously pleased. "Bear that in mind, and we shall have no cause for quarrel. It is in your interest, as well as in ours, to keep these creatures in their place. You may feel that it would make no difference to let one of our enemies go free. But if human beings ever cease to be our servants you would soon learn the difference. These creatures are not capable of living in peace. They would not be content until they were the masters and you and I the servants. Is that what you want?"

"The answer to that question is obvious." Niall could detect a note of impatience in the Master's voice. "But I am unable to follow your reasoning. Why should the release of one young male creature bring about this catastrophe? He does not look particularly dangerous."

"I agree. But that is your mistake. It was he who persuaded your servant Bildo to enter the spider city without permission."

The Master turned his eyes on Doggins. "Is this true?"

Doggins cleared his throat and said uncertainly: "Not as far as I know."

The Master asked Niall: "Is it true?"

Niall shook his head in bewilderment. "No."

The Death Lord said: "Ask him to show you what he is wearing next to his heart."

The Master looked at Niall.

"What are you wearing next to your heart?"

Niall's hand crept inside his tunic and clutched the

thought mirror. The idea of being parted from it filled him
with alarm and dread. But as he felt the eyes of the Master
staring into his own, he took hold of the cord and allowed
the thought mirror to hang outside his tunic.

"Give it to me," the Master said.

And although Niall wanted to keep the thought mirror
more than anything in the world, he knew there was no
question of refusal; the authority of the Master made him
feel like a child. He took the cord from around his neck and
handed it to the Master, who took it in his claw. Then he
looked at the Death Lord.

"It is a simple thought amplifier. We have one in our
history museum." To Niall's immense relief, he handed it
back to him. "Did you use it to influence our servant
Bildo?"

As Niall opened his mouth to reply, he suddenly knew
that it would be impossible to answer with a simple No. He
recognised that the Death Lord could be correct. Doggins
had changed his mind—just as Niall had wanted him to. His
voice reflected his uncertainty as he answered:

"I don't think so. But I'm not sure."

The Master turned his eyes on the Death Lord. "Are you
saying that he did it deliberately?"

"I am saying that he did it. That is why he is dangerous."

As Niall moved back to take his place beside the Death
Lord, he saw something that astonished him. For a brief
moment his eyes met those of the Death Lord, and in that
moment, he found himself looking at Odina. She was still
there inside her body, listening to all that was going on. And
as he again took his place beside her, it seemed to Niall that
he had glimpsed a look of warning and of anguish. For a
moment, he found this revelation so disturbing that he
ceased to pay attention to what was being said. When he

again became aware of their voices, the Death Lord was saying:

"How long will it take your council to decide this matter?"

The Master replied: "I cannot tell you. But it will be soon."

"Good." The Spider Lord seemed about to take his leave. "But let me tell you once again what I have said before. If you decide to release our enemy, it will be a declaration of war."

The tone contained an unmistakable threat. As the Master and the Death Lord stared at each other, Niall became aware that two powerful wills were locked in conflict. He knew— as did everybody else in the room—that the Master was outraged by this attempt to intimidate his council. Yet when the Master spoke, his voice was calm and controlled.

"You are saying that the spiders will declare war on the beetles?"

"I am saying that it is time for the wise to take action."

There was something in the tone of this last word that stirred Niall to alertness, and he started to turn. As he did so, the hands of the Death Lord closed round his throat, and the fingers sank like steel into his flesh. But the moment of alertness had allowed him to move so the hands missed their intended grip; instead of crushing his windpipe, the thumbs were pressing into the flesh below the angle of the jaw. Yet the force was so immense that he felt himself being bent over backwards as if his muscles were paralysed. At the same time, he found himself looking into the eyes of the Death Lord. Once again, he became aware of Odina's presence. And he realised with amazement that she was resisting the will of the Death Lord, and trying to prevent her muscles from obeying his orders to kill.

Then, over her shoulder, he saw the face of the beetle

guard. There was a violent jerk, and he felt his feet leave the ground. The choking grip was suddenly relaxed and he was on his knees, trying to crawl and feeling as if he were swimming. His cheek was pressed to the floor. As his vision cleared, Doggins began helping him into a sitting position.

The first thing he saw was Odina, lying close to the door. She was obviously dead. The body was grotesquely curved, the knees spread out at an angle and one arm twisted underneath her. As Niall flung himself beside her, he saw that her neck was broken; when he took hold of the head and tried to hold it between his hands, it was as loose as if it was no longer attached to the body. The right side of her head had obviously struck the door with enormous force; the right cheek was cut open, and a trickle of blood ran from the corner of her mouth. The beetle guard, who had torn her free, was looking bewildered, as if astonished by his own strength.

Niall tried to stand, but his legs refused to support him. He sat on the floor, his head between his knees, feeling the pulse that beat behind his closed eyelids and hearing the sibilant chatter of the beetles as if it came from another room. When he tried to swallow, the pain made him gasp; it was as if someone had filled his gullet with fragments of broken glass.

The thought of Odina dissipated his self-pity. He used the thought mirror to concentrate his attention and immediately felt better. But he decided to make no further attempt to stand upright. Instead, he stared at the Beetle Lord from his position on the floor.

The Master made a gesture that brought silence. When he spoke, his voice betrayed his anger.

"What you have just witnessed was a deliberate act of treachery. It was also an act of calculated disrespect for our council. He intended to murder a prisoner who was still under our protection. This means that he has forfeited all right to our cooperation. He must realise that we have no alternative except to let the prisoner go free."

Niall tried to speak, but his voice was only a croak. Then he realised that speech was unnecessary; his thought had conveyed his question.

The Master said: "You may go wherever you please. We have decided that we have no right to restrict your freedom. But I would advise you to return to your own country and to remain there. The spiders will now make every attempt to destroy you. And I think it would be a pity if they were allowed to succeed. It would be more than their treachery deserves."

Niall forced himself to rise to his feet, and to make a bow as a gesture of thanks. But as soon as he stood upright, darkness washed over his senses. Doggins caught him as he fell.

BY THE *NEW YORK TIMES*
BESTSELLING AUTHOR OF
DUNE!

FRANK HERBERT
AND BILL RANSOM

"FANS OF THE LATE FRANK HERBERT WILL NOT BE DISAPPOINTED!"

—*Booklist*

___THE ASCENSION FACTOR
  0-441-03127-7/$4.50
___THE LAZARUS EFFECT
  0-441-47521-3/$4.50
___THE JESUS INCIDENT
  0-441-38539-7/$4.95
